THE IMPOSSIBLE JOURNEY

ALSO BY GLORIA WHELAN

GLORIA WHELAN

THE IMPOSSIBLE JOURNEY

 HARPERCOLLINS*PUBLISHERS*

www.harperchildrens.com
Library of Congress Cataloging-in-Publication Data
Whelan, Gloria.
    The impossible journey / Gloria Whelan.
        p. cm.
    Summary: In 1934, thirteen-year-old Marya and her
younger brother, Georgi, set out alone on a long and
arduous journey into Siberia to find their mother after
she and their father are exiled for opposing Stalin.
    ISBN 0-06-623811-0 — ISBN 0-06-623812-9 (lib. bdg.)
    [1. Voyages and travels—Fiction. 2. Brothers and
sisters—Fiction. 3. Political prisoners—Fiction. 4. Siberia
(Russia)—History—20th century—Fiction. 5. Saint
Petersburg (Russia)—History—20th century—Fiction.
6. Soviet Union—History—1925–1953—Fiction.] I. Title.
PZ7.W5718 Im 2003   2002004694
[Fic]—dc21   CIP
                                                      AC

Typography by Alison Donalty
    1 3 5 7 9 10 8 6 4 2
                ❖
          First Edition

For Linda and Frank

CHAPTER ONE

LENINGRAD 1934

Comrade Sergei Kirov was killed on the first day of December. That same night my parents disappeared. The day of Kirov's assassination was a school day and started out like any other. I awoke shivering because my brother, Georgi, who is seven, six years younger than I, had stolen our quilt to wrap himself like a caterpillar in its cocoon. Trying to touch as little of the cold floor as possible, I picked my way across the room. From the window I could see the snow-covered jumble of Leningrad's rooftops and, beyond them, the Neva River. The freezing winds were rushing down from Siberia to lock the Neva in ice.

I pulled on wool stockings and slipped a sweater over my blouse, leaving my hair for Mama to braid. Then I did something wicked. There are people who carefully plan all they do. I'm sure such people never get into trouble. But how do they get anything done? If you think too much about a plan, you think of all the reasons against carrying it out. I rush at things and never make plans. With me everything gets done. The trouble comes later.

I hastily opened a dresser drawer and felt way in the back for the little box I had once discovered there. Inside the box, wrapped in flannel, was a gold locket wreathed with tiny diamonds. I slipped the flannel with the locket into my pocket.

Before I left the room, I poked at the soft lump that was Georgi to awaken him. When he pretended to be asleep, I poked harder. "You have to get up, or we'll be late for school."

"Marya, let me be," his muffled voice came from deep inside the covers. "It's too cold to get up."

I gave the quilt a tug, unrolling Georgi. Ducking the pillows he flung my way, I hurried into the warmth of the kitchen. The tiny kitchen was off our sitting room, where Mama and Papa slept. Down a hall was the washroom, which we shared with the Zotov family. Sergei Ivanovich Zotov was a tall, skinny man like a twist of rope. Olga Pavlovna Zotov was thin like her husband and greedy. If we left our soap in the washroom, it disappeared.

We often found bear hairs in the bathtub, for Mr. Zotov owned a bear cub. You could find Mr. Zotov any day on the Nevsky Prospekt, Leningrad's main street. Holding the cub's leash in one hand and a tin cup in the other, he collected money from the passersby. When a cub grew too large, Mr. Zotov sold it off to a circus. With the money he bought a new cub.

Our warm kitchen was my favorite place. The teakettle was dancing over the fire, the steam from its spout clouding the windows. The day before, Papa had gone to the pawnshop and traded his fur hat to get money for a winter jacket for Georgi.

Mama was setting out sausage and cheese and bowls of hot kasha. "Let me do your hair, Marya," she said. Mama was gentle, never pulling too tightly.

Papa watched. "Spun gold," he teased. "It would take only a lock or two to buy the whole city."

"St. Petersburg is already ours," Mama said. "We have the Summer Garden and the Neva and the Prospekt. It's all there for the taking."

"Katya," Papa cautioned. "Not St. Petersburg! It is now Leningrad. What if the children should call the city St. Petersburg in front of strangers? The man with the mustache might hear of it."

The name of our city had been changed from St. Petersburg to Leningrad after Comrade Lenin died. Lenin was the father of the Communist revolution. "The man with the mustache" was what Papa called Russia's ruler, Comrade Stalin. Papa and Mama despised Comrade Stalin, though this was a dangerous opinion to hold.

Stalin's people had turned my grandmother and her friends out of their land, stealing it and forcing them onto a state farm. There the work was so hard and food so scarce, my grandmother had died.

Georgi stumbled into the kitchen, his sweater inside out, one stocking on and one off. He climbed onto Mama's lap like a fledgling into its nest. "I don't think I should go to school today," he said. "I don't feel so well."

Mama looked closely at him. "Does anything hurt?" she asked.

Georgi thought for a minute. "My ears and my toes."

Mama tried not to smile. She felt his forehead. "You're fine, Georgi. Now let me turn your sweater right side out." She gave Papa a quick, worried look. "Are we having a meeting tonight?"

Papa frowned. "I think we must," he said.

"Misha," Mama warned, "these are such dangerous times. Everywhere, you hear rumors that Stalin is angry with Comrade Kirov for opposing him."

In this year of 1934 Comrade Kirov was the head of the Communist Party in Leningrad and the city's most important man. I had seen Kirov being driven about the city in a big black car. He was a short, square man in a worn black coat who always had bodyguards around him like a flock of crows chasing a small black bird.

Papa said, "There's much about Kirov I don't trust, but what other hope do we have?"

Impatient with all the talk, Georgi helped himself to more kasha, getting porridge all over the floor. Mama reached for the rag, and no more was said about the meeting.

After breakfast Papa left for Leningrad University, where he ought to have been a professor, for he was very learned. Instead he worked there as a janitor, for Papa's parents had been aristocrats. Stalin said all aristocrats were enemies of the people, so Papa was no longer allowed to teach.

Georgi and I went with Mama, who walked us to school on her way to the hospital, where she was employed as an aide. Like Papa, Mama was very educated, but she, too, was an enemy of the people, for her parents had also been aristocrats.

We hurried down our narrow street and turned onto the Nevsky Prospekt. Streetcars clanged back and forth. Tables were set up along the sidewalk where students sold their artwork and others, hungry and desperate for a few kopecks, sold their possessions. Later Mr. Zotov would be there with his bear cub. The cub came from Siberia, and Mr. Zotov had paid a large sum for him so that he could stand on the prospekt and beg money. I loved the fat little bear, whose name was Russ, but it hurt me to see the iron collar about his neck.

A *babushka* with a twig broom was sweeping dirty clumps of gray snow from the sidewalks. A chill wind blew off the icy Neva, making me clasp my coat more tightly and hold on to my hat. No one looked at anyone else. They just stared down at the street or straight ahead. Every day there were arrests, so people no longer trusted one another. The stranger you smiled at today might be the one to report you to the police tomorrow.

Still, Mama could not help smiling. She loved the city. In warm weather she took us to the Summer Garden and told us tales of how elegant women had once strolled along the paths in long white dresses accompanied by handsome officers splendid in their uniforms. She never tired of pointing out the Winter Palace, where she had lived when her mother was lady-in-waiting to the empress. "A thousand rooms," she told us, a dreamy look in her eyes, "and for dinner a platter of roasted pheasants decorated with their own tail feathers."

"Did you have jam for breakfast?" Georgi had asked. There was nothing he liked better.

"Yes, and hot chocolate and sweet buns to go with it," Mama said.

"Did you have children to play with?" Georgi wanted to know.

Mama looked unhappy and would not answer him. The locket hidden in my pocket was shaped like a four-leaf clover. Inside each of the four petals was the picture of a girl. When I had discovered the locket, I had asked Mama who the girls were. Tears came to her eyes and she would not answer me. She took the locket from me and put it back in the drawer, telling me it was a great secret and I was not to touch it again.

Later, Papa, who had seen what had happened, told me Mama had played with the tsar and empress's four daughters: Anastasia, Tatiana, Olga, and Marie. He whispered that something had happened to them that made Mama very sad, but he would not tell me what that something was. It was only later in one of my schoolbooks that I read that the tsar and all his family had been enemies of the state and had been executed for opposing the revolution. I could not believe that the four pretty girls, with their sad, sweet smiles, were enemies of any state.

On this chilly December day Mama did not pause to look at the Winter Palace, or at the mansion, with its tall windows opening onto wrought-iron balconies, where she and Papa had once lived. Instead we hurried on to school, where Mama left us with a kiss.

I took Georgi to his room and headed for my own classroom, where our teacher, Comrade Tikonov, sat at her desk like a queen on her throne. She gave everyone a warning frown, suggesting the queen was sure that we, her subjects, were there only to make mischief. At the front of the classroom, staring down at us, were portraits of Comrade Lenin and Comrade Stalin, the smiles on their faces like the smile on a cat that has just licked up a bowl of cream. Marching across the room was a banner that read LENIN LIVED, LENIN LIVES, LENIN WILL LIVE. Yet everyone knew that for many years Lenin had lain in a coffin in Moscow, stretched out in a glass case like an expensive piece of jewelry.

I placed my assignment, an essay on the leaders of the revolution, on Comrade Tikonov's desk. I had struggled to do it well, but some of the leaders had been exiled from the country and others were in prison or had disappeared, so I had to be careful not to say anything nice about them. I knew that no matter how hard I tried, my work would be returned with angry marks all over it, for I could not keep truth from creeping into my papers.

Comrade Tikonov had taken a dislike to me from the day she had happened to see a picture I had drawn of her with a sour expression and beady eyes. It was exactly like her, but who is happy to see themselves just as they are?

Sitting in the front row was Comrade Tikonov's pet, Svetlana. She was wearing the red scarf of the Pioneers, the Communist young people's organization. Because Svetlana's papa was someone important in the revolution, she turned up her nose at everyone, boasting that her family got to ride about in a big car and spend their vacation at the Black Sea. She bragged that her family could shop in the special store for government officials, and she laughed at my clothes and at the clothes of the other students.

My anger with Svetlana grew inside me like a poisonous mushroom, leading me to do a dangerous thing. Though Mama and Papa had warned me never to mention such things, I had bragged to Svetlana that my mama once lived in the Winter Palace. Svetlana refused to believe me, accusing me in front of the other students of being a liar.

Now I meant to prove I was not a liar. I felt the locket hidden in its bit of flannel.

We began the class as we always did, by standing and facing Comrade Lenin and Comrade Stalin and pledging to uphold the ideals of the revolution. The very worst thing about Comrade Tikonov was that each morning she asked the class to tell her how our families upheld those ideals. If we were quiet for several days and could not tell her how our mamas and papas studied the works of Lenin and Stalin or how they worked at meeting the goals of Stalin's five-year plan, she looked at us suspiciously. I knew that children were encouraged to report parents who were not faithful to the Communist Party. You could have crushed me under a herd of elephants and I would never have reported Mama and Papa.

We were returning to our classroom after lunch when I whispered to Svetlana, "I have something that will prove my mama lived in the Winter Palace."

Svetlana gave me a haughty look. "There is nothing you can show me that will prove it, because it isn't true."

With several of the students looking on, I dug the square of flannel out of my pocket and unwrapped the locket, opening it to show the four-leaf clover, each leaf with its picture of one of the tsar's daughters.

"Now who is a liar?" I demanded. Even as I said the words, a flutter at the pit of my stomach told me I had done something foolish. Svetlana snatched the locket out of my hand. I tried to get it back, but Svetlana was already dashing into the classroom. When I rushed into the classroom after her, Comrade Tikonov had the open locket in her hand, holding it as if it were a snake that would bite her.

In her most imperious voice she ordered, "Marya Mikhailovna Gnedich, come here at once." The look of fury on Comrade Tikonov's face turned me to stone. I couldn't move.

Glaring at me, she demanded, "What are you doing with this? Don't you know these creatures were enemies of the state, living in luxury while the people starved? Have you no shame? This will be reported at once. In the meantime the class will have nothing to do with you. You will move your desk off by itself. I will not have these girls corrupted by such things."

Svetlana gave me a smug smile. What a fool I had been! I huddled down in my seat, miserable and terrified. I felt as if the whole world were staring at me, though in truth most of the girls were sorry for me and kept their heads turned away. I was all the more miserable because I had no one to blame but myself; my pride had led me to act without thinking. Would Comrade Tikonov report the locket to the authorities? What would that mean for Mama and Papa? I would gladly suffer my own punishment a thousand times if it would make no trouble for them.

The end of the day finally came, and everyone crowded out of the classroom, brushing by my desk without a look. Trembling all over, I dared to approach Comrade Tikonov. "Comrade Tikonov," I pleaded, "may I have the locket back?"

With an angry cry she flung it at me so that it fell to the floor. "Take your evil trinket, but you have not heard the last of this."

I picked up the locket and ran from the room. Georgi was waiting in the hall for me, a big smile on his face. "I got an 'excellent' for my drawing of a reindeer." He looked more closely at me. "Why are your eyes all red?"

"Never mind." I grabbed his hand.

All the way home I tried to think what to tell Mama about the locket, for I was sure the school would make a report to her.

It was nearly five o'clock, and along the prospekt the streetlamps were lighted. Because Leningrad is so far north, the night comes early in winter, shutting everyone into darkness as if you were pushed into a closet and the door was closed on you. I had to keep pulling at Georgi, who was trying to fit his boots into footprints he found in the snow.

"This is a giant," he said, pausing at a large footprint. "I can get two of my own boots into just this one."

When at last we reached the apartment, Mama was already preparing supper. Before I could tell her what had happened, she gave us each a kiss and ordered, "Marya, peel the potatoes for me, and Georgi, take your boots off and put on your slippers. Just look at the snow you have left on the carpet."

Glad to gain a little time before I had to tell Mama what had happened, I labored over the potatoes. So as not to be wasteful, I kept the peel so thin you could see through it.

Our supper was ready at six, but Papa was not there. It was nearly seven o'clock when he hurried into the apartment, his face pale, his cap askew. The first thing he did was to sweep Georgi and me up into a crushing hug. Letting us go, he slumped down onto the sofa and drew Mama and Georgi and me beside him.

"Misha! What is it?" Mama asked, her voice hushed as if there were someone listening at the door. "What has happened?"

"Kirov was assassinated this afternoon. The whole city is being turned upside down. No one will be safe. We must be prepared."

"Prepared for what, Papa?" Georgi asked.

I could see from the expression on Mama's face that whatever the thing was, it would be very bad.

"We had no part in it," Mama protested. "You said only this morning that Kirov was our best hope."

Papa shook his head. "All that will make no difference. The police and the soldiers are everywhere. They have the poor fool who shot Kirov in custody, but the rumor is that hundreds are being arrested, though they had nothing to do with Kirov's death. Stalin is using Kirov's death to settle scores with anyone who disagrees with him."

A look of fear came over his face. I had never before seen Papa afraid. "Pavel Andreyovich has been arrested," he said.

Pavel was one of the men who came to Papa's meetings. He was a cheerful, round-faced man with a big laugh who always brought us sweets.

"Marya, Georgi," Mama said, "eat your supper. Papa and I have work to do."

I didn't want to leave Mama and Papa, even for the few steps to the kitchen stove, but Papa said, "Do as you are told, Marya."

I began to spoon out the potato soup, with Georgi watching to be sure I was giving him plenty of bacon. A few feet away from me Mama and Papa were tearing out pages from notebooks and untying the ribbons from packages of letters. The pages and the letters were burned.

Outside the window we could see a torchlight procession winding along the Neva River to the Winter Palace.

"What's happening?" I asked.

"The workers of Leningrad are marching to honor Kirov," Papa explained.

In their haste to burn the notebooks and letters, Mama and Papa forgot the time. It was nearly midnight when Georgi and I went to bed. Georgi fell asleep at once, but I was wide-awake listening to Mama and Papa's whisperings, for they did not go to bed at all.

It must have been two or three in the morning when there was a pounding on the door. I ran into the sitting room, Georgi just behind me. Three policemen burst in, filling the small room. One of the policemen had drawn a gun. What if we were all to be shot like the tsar and his family?

"Mikhail Sergeyevich Gnedich," the policeman with the gun said, "I have an order here for you and your wife. You are under arrest."

"On what charge?" Papa demanded. How brave Papa was to speak up to the man.

"You will hear the charges at NKVD headquarters."

I was sick with fear. The NKVD were the secret police, hated by everyone. The soldiers paid no attention to Georgi and me but set about turning out drawers and pulling books out of the bookshelves. The whole apartment was falling apart around us. I saw a look of terror flash across Mama's face as they emptied the drawer that held the locket. How I wished I could tell her that her secret was safe. But I never got the chance. My taking the locket had not been such a bad thing after all. The discovery of a picture of the tsar's daughters would have been damning evidence that Mama and Papa were truly enemies of the people.

Mama's petticoats and Papa's shirts lay on the floor. Mama's sewing things were all in a heap. The apartment looked like some huge and hungry beast had been foraging for food. When everything had been torn apart, the men motioned to Mama and Papa to put on their coats. Papa did as he was bidden, standing stiff and silent. Mama dashed at us, sweeping us up in her arms. "Look after Georgi," she whispered to me. A moment later Mama and Papa were gone.

CHAPTER TWO

THE SEARCH

Georgi's cries brought our neighbor, Mrs. Zotov. Georgi wrapped himself around her and would not cease wailing.

"Hush, Georgi. Both of you come with me. Quickly." As she led us from the apartment, she gathered up some of Mama's pots and pans and even took one of Mama's petticoats and a shirt of Papa's.

Georgi would not let go of Mrs. Zotov and followed along, clinging to her. I was too frightened to move. She took my arm and pulled me after her. As soon as we were in the Zotovs' apartment and Mr. Zotov had hastily bolted the door, I began to cry.

"Hush," Mrs. Zotov said. "Those policemen were from the NKVD. What if they come back? They must not know where you are. The Lord have mercy on your parents, but they brought it on themselves. I know about those meetings your papa and mama had. In a country like this there must be no going against the leader. You must be invisible, doing nothing to draw attention to yourself. See what their meddling has done. It has made you orphans."

Her words were terrible to me. "What do you mean, orphans? What will happen to Mama and Papa? I'm sure Papa had nothing to do with Comrade Kirov's assassination." I was trembling all over.

Mr. Zotov patted me awkwardly on the head. "There, there. Of course he didn't. Still, he was very foolish."

For a moment, thinking of how Mrs. Zotov had scooped up our belongings, I wondered if it had been the Zotovs who had accused my parents. The Zotovs were greedy busybodies, but I didn't think they would betray Mama and Papa, and surely it was kind of them to take us in. Still, I didn't trust them. First Svetlana had betrayed me and then the police had come. No one could be trusted.

Georgi did not understand all that the Zotovs were saying, but he understood that they were saying things against Papa and Mama. He let go of Mrs. Zotov's apron and leaned hard against me, clutching my arm. He began to wail again.

Mr. Zotov tried to comfort him. "For now you can stay with us, though how we are to feed two more mouths I don't know."

Georgi caught sight of the Zotovs' bear cub in his cage. He wiped his eyes with his sleeve and asked, "Can I pet the bear?"

"Yes, yes," Mr. Zotov said.

A moment later Georgi was on his knees, petting the bear and chattering to him as if Mama and Papa were safe in the next room. It was only later in the night, when Georgi awoke calling for Mama and

Mama did not come, that he began to understand what had happened. Neither I nor Mrs. Zotov could comfort him. I wanted to cry too, but I was the older sister. At last Mr. Zotov, much against his wife's wishes, opened the bear cub's cage. And Georgi, with his arm around the sleeping cub, finally closed his eyes.

The next day was a Sunday. Though Sundays were workdays in the Soviet Union, Mama, Papa, Georgi, and I would get up early and put on our best clothes. We would sneak through the alleys to one of the few churches in Russia where services were still allowed. Afterward as a special treat we would have jam with our bread and a spoonful of butter in our kasha. On this Sunday morning there was no mention of church. After Mr. Zotov left with the bear cub, Mrs. Zotov said, "I suppose we had better take the things that are left in your apartment before someone else gets them."

I stared at her, feeling a terrible coldness, as if I were turning to ice from my toes up. "What will

Mama and Papa do when they get home and there is nothing left?" I asked, afraid of the answer.

Mrs. Zotov would not meet my look. "It will be a while before they return," she said. "In the meantime someone else could grab the apartment and everything in it." As I continued to stare at her, her face became very red. She snapped at me, "I am sure your folks would not want strangers to have their things." With a smug look she added, "If we take you in, those things will be needed." But she made no further move toward our apartment.

I resolved to die of hunger and cold before I lived with such a vulture. I grabbed my coat and went flying down the stairway. Mrs. Zotov called after me, and Georgi cried for me to come back. All I could think of was finding Mama and Papa. Suddenly I knew what I must do. I called up the hallway, "I'm going to NKVD headquarters."

Mrs. Zotov's shout—"You are crazy!"—was the last thing I heard.

Once out on the street I lost my courage. The police were on every corner. I did not see how I was to find the strength to go anywhere near the NKVD. People always spoke of of the NKVD in a whisper. When people passed the wooden building that was its headquarters, they crossed to the other side, keeping their heads down and hurrying by. The official title of the NKVD was People's Commissariat of Internal Affairs. Everyone knew that they were evil men who could swoop down to arrest someone. That someone would never be heard from again.

Then I thought of Mama and Papa and Mrs. Zotov emptying our apartment. I would plead with the NKVD, convincing them that Mama and Papa were good people and innocent of anything bad. I would tell them how no one loved Russia more than Mama and Papa did. I had taken only a step or two when Georgi burst out of the apartment, begging me to wait for him. He held his cap between his teeth. One arm was in and the other arm out of his coat sleeves.

"She stole things from our apartment. I won't stay with her. She'll steal us from Mama and Papa."

"Georgi, please go inside. The place I'm going to is dangerous." Though I pleaded with him, I knew how stubborn Georgi could be.

"If it's dangerous, you won't come back," Georgi said. "You'll disappear like Mama and Papa."

He began to wail. A policeman was walking toward us. "Georgi," I whispered, desperate to avoid the policeman's attention, "if you stop that crying, I'll take you along."

Georgi was quiet, but the policeman kept coming. I saw with relief that he was young, no more than nineteen or twenty. His collar was turned up and the earflaps of his cap pulled down against the cold. He looked from Georgi to me.

"Why is the boy crying?" he asked.

"He's hungry. There is no food at home. I was just going to get him some bread."

Georgi, who never lost a chance for a performance,

turned his large blue eyes upon the soldier and gave him a pitiful look.

The policeman shrugged. "I think all the stores are still closed, but have a look." He walked away.

We passed other policemen, but with Georgi's hand in mine we didn't appear suspicious and we weren't stopped again. It was a chilly two miles to NKVD headquarters, and all the way there my teeth chattered, not from cold but from fear. Would someone even talk with me, and if they did, what was I to say to them? What if they put Georgi and me in jail as well as Mama and Papa? I was desperate to see Mama and Papa again, but what if they had already been sent away? People who were arrested were often shipped to Siberia. Everyone knew of someone who had disappeared without a trace. Or worse, what if they had been executed? My hands were shaking so, I had to let go of Georgi and put them in my pockets. I still had the locket! Suppose they searched me? I thought of throwing it away, yet I couldn't, for I knew how precious it was to Mama.

Two soldiers with machine guns stood at the entrance of the secret police headquarters. "Georgi," I whispered, "you are not to say a word." He nodded his head, and I felt his hand tighten on my arm.

As I approached, the taller of the two soldiers leveled his machine gun at me. Terrified, I turned and ran, pulling Georgi with me. When I thought I had reached a safe distance, I stopped and looked back. The soldiers were laughing. The one who had leveled the gun at us was beckoning to me.

I didn't move. He called to Georgi.

"Come here, little son, and I'll let you look at my gun."

Before I could stop him, Georgi broke away from me and ran to the soldier. I was right behind him. "Georgi, come back."

"I meant no harm," the tall soldier said. "I was only having a little fun. Now, tell us what you are doing here. This is no place for children." The soldier had a little patch on his face like Papa's when he cut himself shaving.

Forgetting all about his promise to be silent, Georgi said, "You have taken away my mama and papa."

The second soldier—whose cap was too large for him, nearly covering his ears—said, "Not us. We stand here all day. We never move. The men who took your parents are inside, and they won't talk with babies."

Georgi kicked the soldier's shin. "I'm not a baby," he said.

Horrified, I pulled him back. "He didn't mean it," I hastily apologized.

"Yes, I did," Georgi insisted.

The tall soldier was laughing again. "I don't know about your mama and papa, my boy, but you'll make a fine revolutionary. Go inside if you like, but I warn you. Don't kick Comrade Yakir in the shins, or you will end up in Siberia." Then he gave Georgi a little push toward the entrance of the building.

Holding my breath, I followed Georgi in. A woman who reminded me of Comrade Tikonov sat before a door like a dragon guarding a cave. She was busy with some papers. Looking up, she glowered at us. "You are in the wrong place," she said. "You can have no business here." I would not have been surprised if she had breathed fire.

I stood very straight and said in a firm voice, "I am here to see Comrade Yakir." I added, "I was sent to see him." In a way that was true, for the soldiers had said, "Go inside."

She folded her lips into a straight line and looked very strict, but she did not tell us to leave. That we had been sent suggested an order from someone, and orders must be carried out. She waited as if she hoped after a moment we might disappear and solve her problem. When we didn't, she got up from her desk.

"This way." She led us down a corridor dark as a tunnel.

Georgi and I clasped hands and followed her. I was holding my breath. Georgi was humming softly, like he always does when he's nervous.

She tapped lightly on a door and waited. A hoarse voice called out, "Don't pound on the door. Come in."

"Comrade Yakir, these . . ." She looked at us, unwilling to say she was bringing children in to see him. "These people say they have been sent to see you." She hurried from the room.

With his fat stomach, little pop eyes, and great semicircle of a mouth that was the shape of a smile but wasn't a smile, the man behind the desk looked like a giant frog.

"Sent here! Who sent you here? I don't talk with children!"

Before he could throw us out, I said, "We've come to find out where you have taken our parents."

His eyes seemed to pop out even more. "So that's it. You are the brats of those who oppose the revolution and side with the assassin of Comrade Kirov. We are turning the whole city upside down to catch such people. I have no time to waste on you."

He was about to call for the dragon when Georgi, his face very red and his hands folded into fists, shouted, "You look like a frog and I hope someone steps on you!"

The frog jumped up. "I'll tell you where your parents are, where we have taken all those responsible for Comrade Kirov's death. To the Kresti Prison, and I hope they stay there until they rot. Now get out of here before I send you there as well!"

In a second we were past the dragon and the two soldiers and out on the sidewalk running as fast as we could.

It was several blocks before we stopped to catch our breath. "Where are we going?" Georgi asked.

"To the Kresti Prison," I answered.

CHAPTER THREE

THE KRESTI PRISON

There were tales of people who had disappeared, never to be heard from again. I would not allow that to happen to Mama and Papa. I had to know where they were. I didn't care what happened to me. Somehow I had to convince whoever was holding Mama and Papa to let them go. I had to make them believe that Mama and Papa would not assassinate a fly, much less Comrade Kirov.

"They'll keep us at the prison," Georgi wailed.

"No they won't. I am going to find Mama and Papa, Georgi, but first I'll take you back to the apartment."

"And leave me there?" Georgi asked.

"Yes, while I go to the Kresti."

Georgi got his stubborn look. "I don't want to stay there by myself. What if you don't come back? Mrs. Zotov won't give me anything to eat but boiled cabbage."

I saw that Georgi would not back down without a scene, which would surely attract attention. "If I let you come with me, you must promise to keep quiet. You're not to get us into more trouble."

As we crossed the city, I was relieved to see that the streets were filling up. In the crowds we would go unnoticed. People were gathered around the billboards where the Leningrad newspaper, the *Leningradskaya Pravda*, was posted. The headline read KIROV ASSASSINATED. The newspaper said that the assassin, Leonid Vasilevich Nikolaev, a thirty-year-old man, had been caught. The people around us read silently, not speaking to one another. Though I could find no mention of other arrests in the newspaper, news of such arrests must be getting around, making everyone afraid.

The NKVD headquarters had looked like a house, while the Kresti looked like a prison. Much as I wanted to find Mama and Papa, I could not get up enough courage to go inside. Here there were no soldiers standing guard, for surely no one would want to break into such a place; it was a place that people went into but did not come out of. I was ready to turn back to the apartment. Even Mrs. Zotov was not as sinister as the sight of the huge building looming in front of us.

Georgi asked, "Are Mama and Papa really in there?"

I nodded.

"I want to see them. Mama needs to mend the hole in my sweater, and she promised to make *blini* for our Christmas Eve dinner, and Papa is going to buy me a present."

I tried to think of a plan, but any plan seemed

foolish, so I took a deep breath and marched through the door.

A soldier, his face unshaven, his tunic unbuttoned, his cap pushed to the back of his head, looked up at us. I could see he was about to send us away.

Boldly I said, "Comrade Yakir at NKVD headquarters sent us here. He said you were to help us to see our parents." Half the phones in Leningrad did not work, and those that did took forever to complete a call. I was betting that so sloppy-looking a soldier would not bother to check on what I was saying.

For a moment the soldier's hand wandered to the phone; then he shrugged and pushed a thick sheaf of papers toward me. "Fill these out," he ordered.

I looked at all the fine print and my heart sank. To get a little time to think, I said, "I have no pen."

He hunted about for a pen, which he reluctantly handed to me, keeping an eye on it all the while I was writing, as if I were there only to steal his pen. There were questions about the addresses of all the places we had lived and birthdates of everyone in the family. I could only guess at many of the answers, but I tried to look as if I knew what I was writing.

Georgi was watching me impatiently. As I scratched away, he announced, "I can read and write. Why can't I write on those papers too?"

At that the soldier's face grew stern. "Hurry up. This is not a kindergarten. I have better things to do. I don't know what Comrade Yakir was thinking of. I've a mind to call him and tell him so." But still he didn't make the call. I think he believed that we would never have been so foolish as to risk coming there unless we had some influence with the authorities. It made no difference that our parents had been arrested; important people were arrested all the time. He must have reasoned that our parents might be let go, and if he did not do what he was told, they would make trouble for him.

After giving the pages I had filled out a quick look, the soldier motioned us to follow him. We were taken to a small room with a cement floor, no window, and a steel door. The room was bare of everything but two chairs, one on either side of a table. Empty as the room appeared, it pressed in on me until I felt I was being crushed, my whole body weighed down with things I imagined might have happened in that room. I didn't know what those things were, but their poison crept from the corners and filled the room. The ghosts of all the people Stalin had arrested were in that room. Georgi must have felt it too, for he left the other chair vacant and edged close to me.

At last the door opened. I reached for Georgi's hand, needing him as much as he needed me. A uniformed woman shoved Mama roughly into the room, slamming the door behind her. We heard a key turn in the lock. A moment later Mama's arms were around us and ours around her. I had never held on to anything so tightly in my life.

When she could catch her breath, she asked, "How in heaven's name did you find me?" A frightened look came over her face. "They haven't arrested you?"

As I was telling her our story, with Georgi helping me along, I was looking at Mama. Her long brown hair, always neatly pinned up, was every which way. Her dress was crumpled, and there was a look of confusion about her. She listened to our story, but I think she hardly heard it. She was only looking and looking at us, continually drawing us to her and covering us with kisses. At last she gave herself a little shake.

"I must speak quickly. I don't know how much time we have. It was dangerous for you to go to the NKVD and even more dangerous for you to come here, but seeing you safe is everything to me. Who is looking after you?"

"The Zotovs have asked us to stay with them."

"God bless them," Mama said. "The worst part of all of this was the worry of what might become of you."

Georgi said, "Mrs. Zotov is stealing things from our apartment."

Mama shook her head. "Let her have them," she

said. "It can make no difference. We will not need them."

Her words frightened me. "Mama," I said, "when will you and Papa come home?"

For the first time Mama cried. "I must tell you the truth. It makes no difference to them that we are innocent. Any day now we will be sentenced and exiled to some town in Siberia—or worse, sent to one of the camps there.

"Imagine, those evil men promised if I said Papa had something to do with the plotting of Comrade Kirov's death, they would let me go back to you. The very men who tore me away from you told me, 'A mother should be with her children.' Marya, Georgi, I would do anything to be with you. How could I choose to leave my own children? But how could I accuse your papa of something he did not do?"

Mama gathered us in her arms. "Listen to me. You must promise to stay with the Zotovs. Somehow we will find a way to let you know where we are. Marya, as soon as we get a letter to you, you must answer us and tell us how you are."

"I can write to you as well as Marya," Georgi said, "but you won't stay away more than a week or two. Otherwise you will miss Christmas. Mrs. Zotov will never make *blini* or buy us presents."

I think Georgi nearly killed Mama with his words. Mama tried to explain. "Georgi, dear, Papa and I don't want to be away. They are making us go away. The place they will send us is very far. It's a journey of many days. I know you are disappointed about Christmas, but you are a big boy now. You will be very brave."

Georgi's face was puckered, and I could see he was fighting his tears. In an angry voice he said, "I won't be brave. I don't want you to go away."

"Georgi," Mama said, "you're breaking my heart. I would give anything to stay here with you." She turned to me and, taking my hands in hers, said, "Marya, you are only a child, but now you must give up being a child. You must take care of Georgi."

Georgi stamped his foot. "I don't want Marya to take care of me. She's too bossy."

Mama put her arms around Georgi and drew him to her. "Listen to me, Georgi. I depend on you to take care of Marya." She looked up at me, giving me a secret smile.

Georgi was quiet now. The idea of being in charge of me was pleasant to him. It almost made him forget that Mama and Papa were going away. He wiped his tears with his fist.

"When can we see Papa?" he asked.

At this Mama became very pale and still. After a moment she said, "Even I can't see him, Georgi. Tonight, when you say your prayers, you must say one for Papa."

The door opened and the same woman strode in. A rough voice ordered us to leave. She reached out and took hold of Mama's arm, but Mama pulled away. She hugged Georgi to her and then gathered me in her arms and whispered, "Marya, be patient with him—he is only a child."

A moment later she was gone. I wanted to run after her. There had not been time enough to say all that had to be said.

The soldier who had given us the papers to fill out came to collect us. "You have to go now," he ordered.

The prison with its dark hallways and iron doors frightened me. Still, as long as Mama and Papa were there, I did not want to leave. Georgi slipped his hand into mine.

"Come, Marya," he said.

I looked down at him. He was looking up at me, and on his face was a protective look. As we left the prison, the soldier called after us, "Be sure to tell Comrade Yakir when you see him that I carried out his orders."

CHAPTER FOUR

THE BEAR

When we returned to the apartment, Mrs. Zotov demanded to know where we had been. "I hope you have not made difficulties for us."

In a bold voice I said, "We have been to NKVD headquarters and to the Kresti Prison." I could not keep a little pride out of my voice.

She was horrified. "How could you do such a thing? It's a wonder they did not keep you there. What were you thinking?" Her face was pale.

I pretended that going to those places was the most natural thing in the world. "Everyone was very nice," I lied, "and we saw Mama."

At that her face softened. "How is she, and what of your papa?"

I told her of the visit. "But we didn't see Papa. Even Mama hasn't seen him." I didn't tell her I planned on returning to the prison.

She was quiet, looking at us as if we were curious beetles to be examined for a moment and then stamped upon.

"You two will be nothing but trouble for us. Perhaps it would be best if you found another place to stay."

I did not want to stay with the Zotovs, but if we left, we would never receive Mama's letter letting us know where she was. I did not dare say that such a letter was coming, for I knew that Mrs. Zotov wanted nothing more to do with my parents. They would think a letter from Mama a very dangerous thing. I took Georgi's hand and headed for the door. Halfway there I turned and said, "Mama said you could have everything in our apartment for keeping

us. Of course, if you don't keep us, we must sell everything to help us pay for somewhere to stay."

Mrs. Zotov's face took on a greedy look, as if
someone had just handed her a box of chocolates.

"Where can two children stay?" she asked. "It
would be very difficult for you to find such a place. It's
a great deal of responsibility for us, and cost as well,
but I can't find it in my heart to send you away. Only
promise me that you will have nothing more to do
with the NKVD or with prisons. You can do your parents no good, and you will do yourselves and us great
harm."

"I promise," I said, though I had no intention of
keeping the promise. After that Georgi and I helped
carry all our possessions into the Zotovs' apartment.
The pots and pans were jumbled together with those
of the Zotovs. The chair Papa settled into each night
to read his books and the table Mama carefully pol-
ished each week were dragged into the Zotovs' apartment and wedged into the vacant spaces. Our quilts

were heaped onto the Zotovs' bed. Our curtains took the place of the worn and ragged ones that had hung over the Zotovs' windows. All I took for myself were my clothes and my paint set.

As we left the apartment, I longed to reach down for the books, which lay on the floor like wounded birds, their pages torn, their covers ripped. Mrs. Zotov stepped over them. "Let the books be," she said. "I am sure they are dangerous. Just see how the police took them apart."

But I could not leave all the books, and when Mrs. Zotov was not looking, I snatched up a few of the ones that Mama and Papa had read to us.

In the Zotovs' apartment Georgi watched as Mrs. Zotov made up beds for me and for him in a space no larger than a closet. All our things were stuffed into a small chest.

"Where will Mama and Papa sleep when they come back from Siberia?" Georgi asked.

At that the greedy look that had been on Mrs.

Zotov's face all the while she was filling her apartment with our things was replaced by a look of true pity.

"It will be a long time before they return, Georgi," she said. "You must not worry about such things. Come, have something to eat. There was some jam in your kitchen, and you shall have it spread thickly on a big piece of bread."

There was a piece of bread for me as well, but the jam on mine was spread very thinly. I was sure Mrs. Zotov did not trust me, for she watched all that I did; certainly I did not trust her.

That evening when Mr. Zotov returned home with his bear cub, he looked about with pleasure at the new furnishings and with disapproval at the two of us sitting on the sofa. "Well, well," he said, in what I was sure he meant to be a cheerful voice, "so our little guests are still here. You are most welcome." Seeing the miserable expressions on our faces, he added, "Come, your mama and papa will be with you soon."

Even Georgi did not believe him. "No they won't,"

he said. "Mrs. Zotov says they will be gone a long while." But in no time at all Georgi was so taken up with Russ, reaching his hand into the cage where the bear was kept and petting the fat cub, that he said nothing more about Mama and Papa.

All through dinner Mr. Zotov was kind to us, hunting about in the borscht for the best bits of beet and potato to ladle into our bowls. Later, though, after he thought we were asleep, I peeked into the sitting room and saw him try out Papa's chair, grinning with satisfaction at how comfortable it was.

In the morning Georgi and I set off for school. The moment Georgi was settled into his classroom, I vanished into the hallway and out the door. It took me a half hour of brisk walking to reach the Kresti Prison. I stood for many minutes at the entrance to the great gray building with its barred windows, trying to get up my courage. *Let them arrest me,* I thought. I wanted to go with Mama and Papa to wherever they were being sent. I did not let myself think of Georgi.

I marched up to the door and entered the prison, where the same soldier, his cap still on the back of his head, his tunic still unbelted, sat at the entrance, scribbling on a piece of paper. When he looked up and saw me, he shot out of his chair.

"You have no business here! We had a call from Comrade Yakir. He said under no circumstances are you to be allowed here."

Taking a deep breath, I managed to get out, "I only want to see my mother for a moment."

"You are too late. Your mother was shipped out to Siberia with a trainload of prisoners this morning."

"But my papa. Where is he? Can I see him?"

The soldier's face became hard as a plank of wood. "No" was all he said, but his way of saying it made me hold on to the desk to keep from sinking to the floor. I felt tears start up.

When he saw my tears, the soldier said in a kinder voice, "Your papa is alive. Now, quickly, get out of here and nothing will be said." His voice hardened once again. "If you are not gone in sixty seconds, I'll call Comrade Yakir, and you will find yourself in prison." He reached for the phone.

I turned and fled.

I did not know where to go with my worry over Papa. I could not tell Mrs. Zotov, who would only scold me for going to the prison. Sleepwalking, I turned toward school. It was nearly noon when I warily opened the door to my classroom. At the sight of me, the whole class became quiet. Comrade Tikonov stared coldly at me.

"So, here is our little troublemaker. Here is the girl who would destroy the revolution and all the great work Comrade Stalin has done. You honor us with your presence rather late in the day. No doubt you have been lolling about in the palace having coffee with the tsar and his family—that is, if they have risen from their graves." At this she gave a cruel laugh. "As you see, your desk is where you put it last week, and there it will stay. As long as you are in this room,

I will see that no other pupil will have anything to do with you. It is people like you who are responsible for Comrade Kirov's death."

I ran from the school. Out on the street I buttoned my coat against the cold and pulled my cap down over my ears. I didn't care about missing school. We had to spend hours learning the speeches of Comrade Stalin. All the books I loved most were forbidden. We studied only Russian scientists. It was Mama and Papa who read to us from the forbidden authors and taught us about the great scientists from other countries.

I wandered along the prospekt, past the Kazan Cathedral and the old Stroganov Palace, past the students selling their paintings, past the women sweeping up the snow. Someone called out, "Marya!"

There was Mr. Zotov with his cap pulled down over his ears and his coat collar turned up against the cold, stamping first one foot and then the other. Russ prowled about at the end of his leash, the wind ruffling his black fur.

"Why aren't you in school?" Mr. Zotov asked.

In my misery I poured out the truth. "My teacher hates me and shames me in front of the other students, and anyhow, I don't learn anything." After making my sad little speech, I saw how foolish I had been. When Mr. Zotov told his wife, she would be more sure than ever that I was a troublemaker. Now that she had all our things, she might turn Georgi and me out onto the street. Anxiously I asked, "You won't tell Mrs. Zotov?"

Mr. Zotov regarded me with narrowed eyes and a sly smile. "You are right to keep your little secret to yourself. I don't believe my wife would want such a mischief-maker under our roof. I'll tell you what: If you stand here and hold on to Russ while I warm myself in the café for a half hour, I'll keep your secret."

I had nothing better to do, and I was fond of the little cub. Mr. Zotov thrust the tin cup at me, first shaking out all but one of the coins into his hand.

"I've left a coin in the cup so that you can rattle it," he said. "Don't stir from this spot. The space belongs to me, and if you move, some pushy student will take it. To make the cub dance, you must pull at the leash like this." He gave several harsh tugs at the leash, and the little bear lumbered this way and that. It was no dance but a desperate shuffle to escape from his tormentor.

As soon as Mr. Zotov was out of sight, I knelt beside Russ and whispered into his ear that I would not pull on his leash. I felt under his collar where the fur was matted and rubbed gently. I scratched behind his ears. Russ made little grunting sounds and swiped playfully at me with his front paws.

A toddler and his mother were watching me. The toddler asked, "Can I pet the bear?" He reached down and patted Russ gingerly on the top of the head and then hurried back to his mother. The mother smiled and dropped a few kopecks into the cup. Some people passed, taking no notice of Russ. A few looked angry, as if they knew the streets of Leningrad were no place for a bear.

A man came by who said he had once lived in Siberia. "The bears there are a thousand pounds," he said, "and when they rear up, they are as big as a house." He shook his head sadly. "To see a wild beast like that on a leash is a terrible thing." He dropped some coins into the cup. "Promise me you will get him a nice fish for his dinner." With one more regretful look at the bear he walked away.

The half hour stretched into an hour and then another. I hardly noticed the time passing or the cold breezes off the Moyki Canal. I could think only of Mama being sent away and not knowing what had become of Papa. I had to find them, but I did not know how to take the first step.

My nose was like a chip of ice. I couldn't feel my toes. Only my hands were warm, for I kept burying them in Russ's fur. At last a young man in the neighboring stall took pity on me. He had started a small fire in a little metal burner.

"You with the bear," he said. "Warm yourself."

Gratefully I held my hands and face near his fire.

"My name is Igor. What's your name?" he asked.

"Marya." I stole a look at him. He was thin, with high cheekbones and eyes that turned up at the corners. His long black hair hung about his shoulders. His black jacket was nearly green with age, and his fingers poked out of his gloves.

"That old man has left you to stand in the cold while he has his vodka in a warm café. Why don't you let that poor beast go and take off?"

"My brother and I live with that man and his wife. Anyhow, what good would it do to let Russ go? He couldn't get along by himself in the city, and someone would only steal him. They might even eat him." Mrs. Zotov had poked Russ's fat belly and announced he would make a nice stew.

I looked at the paintings Igor was trying to sell. They were cheerful pictures of neat wooden houses in a green and leafy countryside. Smiling peasants stood about grinning. The trees were full of apples and pears, and the fields were golden with grain. There were fat geese and woolly sheep. This reminded me of Mama's description of the countryside around the Oaks, the country house where Mama had gone as a child.

"Your pictures are very pretty," I said. But I was thinking of how my grandmother and her friends had been forced from their land.

"I hate the pictures," Igor said. "The truth is, the peasants in the countryside who are not already dead are starving. These pictures are nothing but a lie."

"Then why do you paint such pictures?" I tried to make my own pictures as honest as I could.

"I paint the pictures to sell them, of course. Who would want to hang a picture of starving peasants on his wall?"

"There are things to paint besides starving peasants," I said.

"What do you know about painting?"

"I paint a little myself." I gave a quick look to see if he was laughing at me, but he only looked surprised.

"What training have you had?"

"Only in school, but there I had to paint what I was told."

Igor said, "It was the same with me. I was a student at the Leningrad Art Academy. Two years ago I was expelled from the school because I refused to paint happy workers." He gave me a cynical smile. "Now I paint something just as impossible, happy peasants."

For someone who was out of favor with the government, Igor was very careless. He said what he pleased.

When he learned Mama and Papa had been arrested after Kirov's death, he said, "That is just like Stalin. He blames everyone else for what he has done himself."

I looked hastily about to be sure no one had heard

him. "What are you saying?" I whispered. "Stalin and Kirov were friends."

"Nonsense. Kirov was Stalin's competition for the head of the Communist Party. Now Stalin has gotten rid of Kirov, and he is using Kirov's murder to round up anyone who supported Kirov."

I stared openmouthed at Igor. Something about Igor's courage made me confide in him. "They told me Mama has been exiled to Siberia, but they would not tell me where Papa is. Why should they not tell me?"

He gave me a pitying look. "What is your papa's name?" he asked.

"Mikhail Sergeyevich Gnedich." My voice shook a little as I spoke the name.

"I'll see what I can find out," he said. "I know people who have contacts in the prisons." He began to pack up his paintings. "It will be too dark to sell pictures soon." With that he was gone.

The early-afternoon sun began to disappear, so it was like twilight when Mr. Zotov returned. Roughly he snatched the cup from my hand and reached for Russ's leash. He counted the coins.

"Not too bad, but you could have done better."

"One coin is for a fish for Russ. A man gave it specially."

"Waste a fish on that bear? Don't be a fool. Marya, I'll say nothing to my wife about your skipping school. This will be our little secret. Be here tomorrow morning and you can help me out again."

I ran all the way to the school so I would be in time to pick up Georgi. He had a big smile, and a star was pasted on his forehead.

"I was the only one who could name five of Russia's natural resources." He began to call them off. "Lumber," he said, "and gold and oil and . . ."

I saw that for a moment he had forgotten the terrible thing that had happened to us, and I envied him.

After I had washed and dried the dinner dishes, I got out my paints. There were no cheerful cottages with flowers for me to copy. I looked about the room.

There was Russ snoozing with his muzzle between his paws. I sketched him and then took up my brush.

Mrs. Zotov watched me work. "You have that cub to the life," she exclaimed. "We'll hang your picture on the wall."

Hastily I said, "It's for school. It's my homework for art class."

Mr. Zotov gave me a sly look. He knew very well there would be no school and so no homework, but we had made a bargain. All he said was, "You could get a good sum for that paint set."

The next day, clutching my little painting, I took Georgi to school and hurried on to the spot where Igor had been, anxious to hear if he had any word of Papa. Mr. Zotov was expecting me. At once he handed me Russ's leash. "Don't forget to rattle the cup," he said, "and pull the bear's leash to make him dance." He hurried toward the warmth of the café.

A few minutes later the student appeared. I hesitated for a moment and then brought out my picture of Russ. He smiled. *"Molodyets!"* he said. "Well done! Put it with mine. No one will buy pictures from a child. If it sells, you will have the money."

I was angry at being called a child, but I put my picture with his. Minutes later a man came by and studied first Russ and then the painting of the cub. "How much do you want for that?" he asked Igor.

"Two rubles," Igor said.

I wanted to say that that was too much. The man would walk away. Instead the man offered half the amount. Back and forth they bargained. At last the man left with the picture. Igor handed me a hundred and fifty kopecks.

"I'm keeping twenty kopecks as my commission," he said.

"You're welcome to them," I told him. "I would never have asked for so much."

"Then you would have been a fool."

"Have you found anything out about my papa?" I asked.

"Tell me his name again."

"Mikhail Sergeyevich Gnedich, the same as yesterday."

He nodded. "I just wanted to be sure. Since Kirov's assassination they have no rules, no trials."

"What does that mean?"

"It means they do as they please." He paused. "From what I hear, your papa has been sentenced to hard labor and sent to a camp somewhere in Siberia where the prisoners mine coal." When he saw my expression, he took me gently by the shoulders and, looking into my face, said, "It could be worse. There were twenty-five executions yesterday."

CHAPTER FIVE

A LETTER FROM DUDINKA

By the end of December the newspapers announced that Kirov's assassin had been found guilty. He had been executed and, along with him, his friends and many of his relatives. I had never told the Zotovs what had happened to Mama and Papa, letting them think my parents were still in Leningrad and might return for us at any time. As the days wore on, I saw that Mrs. Zotov was beginning to resent the food she put on our plates.

Each day was the same. I took Georgi to school and stood all day with Russ on a leash, listening to Igor's bitter words. In the afternoon I hurried home with Georgi, praying for a letter from Mama and Papa.

I did one bad thing. Each day I kept a few coins from the cup. At first I had asked Mr. Zotov if he would pay me a wage for taking his place.

"What?" he said. "We give you and your brother a warm bed and feed you, and you want money besides?"

After that I kept the coins, buying only a little watercolor paper and hiding the rest of the coins among my stockings, where I hid the locket and my earnings from the paintings I had sold with Igor's help.

Christmas came with no presents and no celebration. When we awoke on Christmas morning, we eagerly dressed for church, but church was not allowed.

Mrs. Zotov said, "They have spies who write down the names of everyone who goes into the church. If you go, it will get us in trouble."

Georgi and I were so angry, we spent the morning

singing Christmas carols at the top of our voices:

> *Father Christmas, Father Christmas steals*
> *about on Christmas Eve.*
> *Father Christmas, Father Christmas at the*
> *window cakes will leave.*
> *Father Christmas, Father Christmas, come*
> *this Holy Night, we pray.*
> *Father Christmas, Father Christmas came*
> *and brought us Christmas Day.*

When our voices gave out, we went outside and found a branch of a tree, which we brought inside. I painted pictures of Father Christmas and his reindeer. Georgi cut the pictures out, and together we hung them on the twigs of the branch. Georgi was happy with it, but it looked so sad to me that I resolved that by next Christmas I would find Mama and Papa.

Russ was growing. When he became too large to handle, I knew, Mr. Zotov would sell him to a circus and buy a new cub. I was already having trouble hanging on to Russ; still, I hated the thought of seeing him go. We had become friends. I had taught him to dance by rewarding him with bits of fish from the table. Mrs. Zotov scolded me for my extravagance, but Mr. Zotov took my side, for he could see there were more coins in the cup when the bear performed.

"Let her teach him to dance. Besides, the bear must have a treat now and then," he said to his wife.

"Why should the bear have a treat when we have hardly enough for the pot?" she asked.

"Because," her husband answered with a wink at me, "a clever bear brings in more money."

In the winter evenings Georgi and I curled up beside Russ, enjoying the bear's warmth, for it was always cold in the Zotovs' apartment. While Russ snoozed, I painted a picture, always telling Mrs. Zotov that it was homework. Sometimes I painted Georgi, sometimes the rooftops I saw from the window.

Georgi pleaded, "Paint Mama and Papa."

It took me several days, and I earned no kopecks on those days. When I had finished the portraits, Georgi said, "You aren't going to take those to school?"

"No, Georgi. We'll keep them."

I began another painting of Russ, who was my most popular subject, always selling when the rooftops often did not. There were several pictures of rooftops on the Zotovs' walls.

Mrs. Zotov insisted, "Marya, now you must do pictures of Mr. Zotov and me, and you must tell your teacher to let you bring them home like you brought home all the rooftops."

I didn't want to waste time on something I could not sell, but I didn't dare anger Mrs. Zotov, so I set to work.

I had bragged to Igor that paintings need not be dishonest, but now I made two dishonest paintings, for how could I let the Zotovs see how greedy and dishonest I thought them?

Winter passed quietly, but no letter came from Mama. The ice began to melt on the Neva. One morning I saw ducks swimming in open water. People no longer wrapped themselves from head to toe. Feather beds were given their spring airing. Porch stoops were cleared of their winter grime.

There were mild days when the sun was warm and the breezes gentle. It was almost pleasant standing on the prospekt now. When he saw the pleasure I took in the mild days and the street sights that meant spring, Igor laughed at me.

"Have you forgotten already why you are standing here, Marya?"

Of course I had not forgotten. No minute of the day went by without my thinking of Mama and Papa and praying for some word from them. Still, when you were miserable, spring was better than winter. Certainly it was warmer.

Igor's paintings were getting more and more cheerful. The peasants' smiles grew wider, the geese got fatter, the trees had more green leaves. As the pictures became happier, Igor grew more and more glum and more careless with his words. "I've heard stories of the camps in Siberia where they force the prisoners to mine coal in freezing weather with no shoes or gloves. They don't care. For every prisoner who dies, there are a hundred more arrested to take his place."

When he saw the frightened look on my face, he apologized. "Never mind, Marya. Your father will be one of the lucky ones who will come back."

His words did nothing to reassure me. I could not get the picture of the miserable prisoners out of my head. The next day Igor did not appear. I had to sell my own paintings, and since I was too shy to bargain, I got only half of what Igor would have. When I asked one of the other students where Igor was, he shook his head. When I pressed him, he looked around carefully. "Igor talked too much. I heard he was arrested yesterday."

After that I began to give up hope. The final blow came at the end of April, when Mr. Zotov brought home a tiny, scrawny cub at the end of the leash where Russ should have been.

I had no heart for the new cub. I stood all day, too miserable to rattle the cup. The new bear was either too stupid or too young to learn to dance. At the end of the day there was so little money in the cup, I was afraid to take even a kopeck for myself.

Just when I thought I could not get through another day, the letter came. Mrs. Zotov was holding it in her hand when I arrived home. Though it was addressed to Georgi and me, she had opened it. Now she held it out, a worried look on her face. It was all I could do to keep from snatching it from her hand. I wanted to take it someplace where I could read it by myself, but there was no place to go. At last, with shaking hands and with Georgi trying to see the words over my shoulder, I read the letter.

My very dearest Marya and Georgi,
I am living in a little hut in the town of

Dudinka near the Yenisey River. The river gives me fish, and when it is warmer, I hope to start a little garden with potatoes and cabbage.

Before I left, I learned the terrible news that Papa was sentenced to a camp in Siberia, but I could not discover where it is. I can hardly bear to be separated from him. I have heard nothing from him and can only pray that he is well. You must remember him every night in your prayers.

I came first by railway and then by steamer, and every mile I traveled from Leningrad broke my heart, for it took me farther and farther from you and from Papa.

There is no moment of the day that I do not think of you. Only my love for you encourages me to go on. All through this cruel winter the thought of you has warmed my heart and given me hope.

*I have been sentenced to remain here in
Siberia for three years. I must regularly
report to an officer in the town. Even if I
wished to leave, there would be nothing to
escape to but endless ice fields and tundra.*

*Please tell the Zotovs how grateful I am,
and write at once to let me know how you
are. I send a thousand kisses and all my love.*

Mama

Three years! I would be sixteen, and Georgi ten.
Mrs. Zotov was thinking the same thing, for she said,
"Three years is a very long time." I could tell from the
pinched expression on her face that she was considering
all the breakfasts and dinners she would have to give
us. Mama and Papa's few possessions would never
pay for all that. Of course she did not know I was
doing her husband's work for him.

I wrote at once to Mama. In my letter I tried to
sound cheerful, so that I would not add to her worries,

but from the first moment I had seen the address on the letter, I had determined to go to Mama. I had no plan. I did not care how far it was or how long it took. All I knew was that I must start out. Anything would be better than standing on the street hanging on to a bear and putting up with Mrs. Zotov's resentful looks at every morsel of food Georgi and I put into our mouths. I was sure she would have been rid of us long since if it hadn't been for Mr. Zotov, who was quick to take our part, for I was making it possible for him to spend his days in the café.

I still had my schoolbooks. As soon as I had a minute to myself, I opened my geography book to a map of Siberia. It took up a double page and stretched for thousands of miles. I did not know where Papa was, but I found Dudinka. Dudinka. The name had the sound of a stone dropped into the water. You could even hear the little splash at the end. It was a name that could only be far away. Dudinka was near the mouth of the great Yenisey River, close to where the river emptied into the Arctic Ocean. There was a railway that went from Leningrad across Russia and over the Ural Mountains to the Yenisey River. I began to trace a path. The railway journey would take several days. I figured that the distance from the railway stop to Dudinka was at least a thousand miles. An impossible distance! I carefully tore out the map. Even that small act made me feel as if I had started the journey.

I would have to find money to get a railway ticket and a steamship ticket. The railway would take me to the Yenisey River. Once I reached the river, I could take a steamship as Mama had.

Though he was lying beside me, I did not think of taking Georgi. How could I afford two railway tickets and two steamship tickets and food for two people on the journey? Georgi would be safe with the Zotovs. Surely they could find food enough for one small child. I put out of my mind Mama's words, "You must take care of Georgi." All I could think of was finding Mama.

The next morning I left Georgi off at school and hurried to the rail ticket office off the prospekt. A ticket from Leningrad to the town of Krasnoyarsk on the Yenisey River would cost every ruble I had, leaving no money for food or a steamer ticket. I walked sadly away, thinking I would have to wait a year. The new cub was growing, and I could teach him to dance. I would paint more pictures and save every kopeck I could.

Mr. Zotov was waiting impatiently for me. "Where have you been? You have kept me here an hour. As it is, I am going to be late for my appointment. If I lose the opportunity, it will be your fault." With that he flung the cub's leash at me and stalked off.

I was so intent on my plans, I thought no more of Mr. Zotov's "opportunity" until that afternoon, when he came to relieve me of the bear.

"Well, Marya, my luck has turned. Here are a few kopecks for you to buy a sweet or two. Your days of standing here are over."

"What do you mean?" I asked. I tried not to show my alarm.

"The circus where I sell my cubs is looking for someone to care for the animals—feed them and clean up and such. They're taking me on. No more standing on the street rattling a cup. It will be rubles, not kopecks, from now on. Run along, but say nothing to my wife. I want to surprise her."

When she heard the news from her husband that evening, Mrs. Zotov could not stop smiling. "More money, and we get rid of the bear. At last the apartment will no longer smell like a zoo." She looked at Georgi and me as if we too were making the apartment smell like a zoo. "Sometimes, Marya," she said, "I think you and Georgi might be happier where there are other children your age."

I saw the calculating look on her face. She wanted to put us into an orphanage. This time Mr. Zotov said nothing in our favor. The bear cub was to be sold the next day, and he would begin his work at the circus.

He no longer needed me.

I had enough money for a single railroad ticket, but I knew I could not leave Georgi behind to be sent to an orphanage. There had to be some way to get money for Georgi's ticket. After everyone was asleep, I took my little store of coins from my chest and counted them in the dark, for I knew each coin by feel. I hoped that somehow they had increased like a brood of rabbits, but it was only the same meager amount. As I hid them away among my stockings, I felt the locket in its flannel.

In the morning I hurried to the pawnshop where Papa had pawned his fur hat and the last bits of Mama's jewelry. I had gone there once with Papa, and I recognized the man behind the counter. He was always friendly to Papa, for he was happy to have the things Papa brought. Now he gave me a quizzical look.

"What brings you here, young lady? Has someone sent you with something for me? I hope it isn't a watch.

I must have every watch in Leningrad. I don't see how people tell the time."

I hesitated, wondering if I could trust the man. I remembered Comrade Tikonov's fury when she saw the locket. Perhaps the man would call the authorities and have me arrested as an enemy of the people. I looked about. We were alone in the store. I took the locket carefully from its flannel and laid it upon the counter.

The man smiled. I could see he liked the locket. He examined it closely. "A treasure made by the great jeweler Fabergé," he said. He opened it. "No pictures?" he asked. I shook my head. The pictures of the four girls were in my pocket.

"There is no market in this city for something like this. People want food, not fancy jewelry."

My heart dropped into my stomach. I was about to reach for the locket.

"However, they like these little baubles in Europe." He began to lay rubles onto the counter.

There were enough for another railway ticket and for food to keep Georgi and me from starving. I snatched up the rubles and ran out of the shop before he could change his mind.

At the rail ticket office, much to the astonishment of the agent I counted out the money for two tickets. He looked hard at the money, as if there might be something wrong with it, but in the end he gave me the tickets. The tickets were very long, for they would take us on a long journey. I folded them carefully and tucked them well into my pocket. There was no money left for steamship tickets, but I was determined to start out. From the map I knew that once we reached the river, we had only to follow it. To cover more than a thousand miles to Dudinka in just three months' time, we would have to walk fifteen miles a day. What's more, we would have to leave at once if we meant to get to Dudinka by fall and the start of the Siberian winter.

That night Mrs. Zotov prepared a fine dinner. I

thought it was to celebrate Mr. Zotov's first day at his new job, but I was wrong.

"Come, Georgi, have another bit of ham. Marya, I made the potatoes with dill and sour cream, just as you like them." For dessert there was a big bowl of stewed fruit, the apricots and prunes glistening in the syrup like jewels.

After dinner Mrs. Zotov waved us away from the sink. "No, no. Tonight I'll take care of the dishes. You pack your clothes."

Georgi and I looked at each other. For a moment I thought she had found out I had been to the railroad office and that she could see right through my pocket to the tickets.

Making her voice cheerful, Mrs. Zotov said, "I have found the perfect children's home for you. There is even a little yard where you can play about. There are classes for Georgi, and for you, Marya, instruction on cooking and housecleaning. The home furnishes cleaning women for the office buildings in Leningrad, so one day you will have a job."

I could do nothing but stare at her. She bristled under my angry and silent look.

"They will teach you manners as well," she added.

"I don't want to go to an orphanage," Georgi said. "Mama gave you all our things to keep us."

"And keep you we did," Mr. Zotov said. "Haven't we been feeding you? The bits and pieces from your parents are worth nothing. They have only cluttered up our apartment."

"Then why do you sit on our papa's chair every night?" Georgi demanded.

Mr. Zotov sprang out of the chair. His face was an angry red and his voice harsh. "We will have no more discussion. The two of you pack your things. You go to the children's home in the morning."

Georgi kept looking at me, waiting for me to say we would not go. I saw his look of disappointment at my silence. I knew he felt I had let him down, but I said nothing because my mind was busy. We must escape that night. If we delayed our departure until we were in the orphanage, it would be impossible to get away. Georgi and I might even be in separate buildings.

We would wait until the Zotovs were asleep, and then we would leave. If they heard us moving about, they would think we were going to the bathroom in the hallway. I looked at the remainder of the ham on the kitchen shelf. Beside it there was some cheese and a package of dried apricots and prunes.

I pushed Georgi into our tiny, closetlike room.

In an accusing voice he asked, "Marya, why didn't you say something?"

"Listen," I whispered, "we are going to run away and find Mama."

Georgi's eyes grew large, and he gave me a huge smile. "When?" he asked.

"Tonight," I said. "But Georgi, it will be very hard. We have a long railway journey and not much money for food. And Georgi, we will have to walk a thousand miles."

All Georgi heard was "railway journey." His face lit up. "We are going on a train?"

"Yes. Now hush and pack your things in your suitcase. Take only what you need. And remember, appear unhappy when you are with the Zotovs."

From time to time one of the Zotovs looked into our cubbyhole to see what we were doing. They were reassured as we packed the small suitcases that had belonged to Mama and Papa. As he said good night to us, Mr. Zotov handed a ruble each to Georgi and me.

"You are good children, after all," he said.

Georgi and I gave him a very sad look. Some devil made me ask, "Will you come to see us?"

He was taken aback. I could see the idea had never entered his head, but he assured us, "Yes, yes. Yes, indeed. Very often, and we will bring you treats."

I thought the Zotovs would never go to bed. They sat up late into the night. I had left our door open a bit and could hear them talking about Mr. Zotov's new job and what the extra money would mean to them.

Then there were only whispers, and I knew they were talking of us.

It was long after midnight when Georgi and I heard the Zotovs' familiar snoring. I stuffed a blanket into each of our suitcases. Georgi and I quietly slipped into our coats. Tiptoeing into the kitchen, I snatched the ham, the cheese, and the packages of fruit. My suitcase had a pleasant full feeling. We crept out of the apartment, down the stairway, and into the night.

CHAPTER SIX

BY TRAIN INTO SIBERIA

But for a dark figure in a doorway or a shadow rounding a corner, the streets were deserted. We hurried down the Nevsky Prospekt and across the Anichkov Bridge with its great bronze horses to the Moscow Railway Station. The station clock said three in the morning, but already there were passengers awaiting the early trains. Every few minutes a voice announcing the departure or arrival of a train boomed out over the loudspeakers, startling Georgi, who was hanging on to me as if he were slipping over a cliff and I were the rock he was grasping.

Our train left for Moscow at six A.M. From

Moscow we would change to the Trans-Siberian Railroad. The journey seemed so mysterious and so difficult, I did not see how to take the first step. So strange were the clouds of steam that nearly hid the trains, so loud was their rumble as they came and went, and so sharp the odor of coal that filled the station, I was almost resolved to hurry back to the Zotovs' apartment, replace the food, and crawl into bed. How could the orphanage be worse than this trip into the unknown?

Across the waiting room I saw a woman leaning against a man. The man's arm was around the woman. Two boys were curled up asleep next to the couple. The boys were Georgi's age and looked like twins. The man was staring at us in a curious but friendly way, a smile on his lips. A friendly face in all that strangeness drew me. Pulling Georgi after me, I settled down on a bench next to the man and his family.

The man watched me for a moment and then

quietly asked, "What are the two of you doing here all alone?"

I was afraid of falling into a trap. I could not trust anyone. How could I tell him the truth? He might turn us over to the authorities. We would be arrested for running away and put not into an orphanage, but into a prison.

Hastily I said, "We are waiting for our parents. They will be here at any time."

The man did not miss Georgi's amazed look at my lie. Still, the smile stayed on his lips. His wife had awakened and was looking curiously at us now. The couple were about the age of our parents. The man had a beard and little wrinkles about his eyes. He was as chubby as Russ. The woman wore her hair twisted around her head in an old-fashioned braid. Though she smiled at me, there was a sadness behind the smile. The twins looked as much like each other as a reflection in a mirror.

"My name is Dr. Glebov," the man said, "and this

is my wife, Olga, and my boys, Nikolai and Yuri. What are your names?"

"I'm Marya, and my brother is Georgi."

"Where are you going?"

Because I could think of no other answer, I said, "To the Yenisey River."

His eyebrows shot up. "That's a long journey." He looked at the tickets I clutched in my hand. "You must be taking the same trains we are, but our journey is not so far. We get off the train at the Ob River."

Mrs. Glebov offered, "Can I give you some *makivnek*?"

"No thank you," I said. "We have our own food." I worried that I had been too quick to respond to their friendly gestures. How did I know that they were not some sort of government spies?

Georgi had been staring at the twins, paying no attention to what we were saying; but at the mention of *makivnek* he pricked up his ears. "I'll have some, please," he said.

I frowned at him, but the woman only smiled and reached into a basket for two pieces of cake, which she handed us. I wanted to refuse, but it had been a long time since dinner, and the cake had almonds and raisins and a thick layer of frosting, so before I could stop myself, I was eating it.

With the cake safely in his stomach Georgi curled up next to me and fell asleep. I tried to keep awake, but my eyelids kept drooping. Dr. Glebov leaned across and said, "Sleep if you like—I'll wake you in plenty of time for the train." He said nothing about our parents arriving.

Gratefully I closed my eyes, and in a moment, worn out by all my worry, I was asleep.

It seemed only a second later when Dr. Glebov shook me gently awake. "They have called our train," he said. "Do you have your passports ready?"

I sat up, startled. "What do you mean?"

"You cannot go anywhere in this country without a passport. If you don't have one, they will never let you on the train."

Tears spilled out of my eyes. With no more thought of caution I poured out our story. "My parents have both been arrested and sent to Siberia. My papa has been sent to a coal mine, and my mama has been exiled to Dudinka." I showed him the letter with her address. "We are going to her. If we stay here, they will put us in an orphanage."

The Glebovs appeared amazed at our story. "It's a long way from where the railroad puts you off to the town of Dudinka," the doctor said. "Do you have tickets for the steamship? And how will you take the steamship with no passport?"

"We're going to walk."

"That's impossible!" Mrs. Glebov said.

"No," I said. "We'll have three months. I know we can do it if we can just get on the train that will take us to the river."

Dr. Glebov looked at us for a long moment. "Listen to me, both of you. I have a family passport that includes my children but does not name them. Stay close to me and remember that for now your last name is Glebov."

He awoke the twins, and the six of us pushed our way into the crowd that was headed for the train. Dr. Glebov held out his passport for the conductor, who looked at the twins and then at Georgi.

"You have three the same age?" he asked in a suspicious voice.

"Only two." The doctor laughed. "This one"—he pointed to Georgi—"is a year younger, but he grows like a weed."

Dr. Glebov's easy laughter seemed to assure the conductor, and he said no more.

As we climbed onto the train, I saw Dr. Glebov looking at some boxcars attached to the trains. Soldiers were loading chained prisoners onto the cars. On the roof of each boxcar was a soldier with a machine gun. The doctor looked quickly at me and urged us onto the train. The sight of the prisoners had sent my heart into my shoes. I wanted to ask if Papa had been sent that way, but Dr. Glebov hurriedly guided us to a compartment. "Stay here with us and you'll be safe," he said.

Georgi was still staring at the twins. At last he asked them, "How do you know which you are?"

They stared back at Georgi. One of them, who turned out to be Yuri, said, "We look in the mirror." He was laughing.

"Our mama knows, and she tells us each morning," Nikolai said. He was grinning at Georgi.

"Shame on you boys for teasing Georgi," their mother said. She turned to Georgi. "They know the same way you know who you are. Boys, show Georgi the puzzle you got for Christmas."

They brought out a puzzle board with a little figure to be propelled through a complicated maze. "Bet you can't guess how he should go," Yuri challenged Georgi.

Together the three boys bent their heads over the

board. When the doctor saw that they were busy with the puzzle, he asked in a quiet voice, "Do you know the name of your father's camp?"

I shook my head.

"That's a pity. I was hoping against hope it might be the camp at Vorkuta. That's where I am being sent."

"Have you been arrested?" I asked. "Are you being sent to exile?"

"No, no," he replied. "I am being sent by the government to be the doctor at the camp there."

A chill traveled up my spine. I had trusted a man who was working for the government. I remembered the terrible things Igor had said about the coal-mining camps. "They force the prisoners to mine coal in freezing weather with no shoes or gloves," he had said. Now this man was going to be part of such a camp. I pulled away from him.

He watched me closely. "I know what you are thinking, Marya. You believe I am a part of the evil that is done in the camps."

Mrs. Glebov reached over and laid her hand on his. "Anatoly," she said. "We have gone over this a thousand times. Stop punishing yourself. What else could you do?"

"The government ordered me to go," Dr. Glebov said. "If I had not obeyed, what would have become of my family? Even so, I might still have disobeyed them. I decided to go for another reason. I pray that I will be able to make a difference in the camp. I have thought it all through. I can insist the prisoners do not work when they are ill. I can demand that they are given enough food for the hard work they do. I will find ways to make things easier for the men."

There was not much conviction in the doctor's voice, but there was much hope. The differences he would be able to make were very small and the camps very evil; still, I hoped that Papa would be at the doctor's camp.

I jumped as our compartment door was pushed open, but it was only an old *babushka* with a pot of tea.

The doctor bought cups for all of us. I opened my suit-case and started to offer the bread and ham to the Glebovs. The twins looked hungrily at the ham, but Dr. Glebov said, "No, no, you must save that. You have a long journey ahead of you. While you are with us, you will share our food."

I began to think the prisoners at Dr. Glebov's camp would be lucky to have him.

Like Georgi, the twins had never been on a train. So fascinated were the three boys with the pass-ing scenery that we had to hang on to them so they wouldn't fall out of the window. Though I tried to be more reserved than the boys, it was my first train trip as well. I, too, longed to hang out the window, for everything we passed was new and strange to me. I might have been running through a museum, seeing picture after picture over my shoulder.

While the train rushed along on its way to Moscow, I heard the Glebovs' story. The head of the Communist Party at the doctor's hospital had discov-ered that Dr. Glebov had an American medical journal and, even worse, was trying a new treatment written up in the journal.

"It makes no difference to the Party if you can save lives," the doctor said. His voice was bitter. "Stalin has declared America the enemy, and anything American bad. They dismissed me from the hospital and packed me off to Siberia."

Then I told about Russ and the Zotovs. Mrs. Glebov shook her head sadly. "At least we are together with our children," she said. "What must your parents be feeling?"

It was early evening by the time the train pulled into the station in Moscow. Georgi and I had been up almost all night and traveling all day, but the sights from the train window had kept us awake. Now, here we were in Russia's great city. "Will we get a glimpse of St. Basil's Cathedral and the Kremlin?"

Dr. Glebov frowned. "No, nor do I want to see the Kremlin."

I knew what he meant. The Kremlin was home to Comrade Stalin. I shivered.

"The sooner we leave Moscow, the better," Dr. Glebov said. He shepherded us the short distance between the Leningrad Station and the Yaroslavski Station, where the next morning we boarded the train that would take us to Siberia's Yenisey River. From there Georgi and I would begin the unknown part of our journey. Whenever the thought of what lay ahead became too frightening, I told myself that with each mile we would be closer to Mama.

We were furnished with rough blankets, and there was a washroom at the end of the car. It was very cozy, and I almost wished we could stay forever in the safety of the train with the Glebovs there to watch over us. It was only when I thought of Mama that I wished for the train journey to end so the next journey could begin.

Mrs. Glebov called out in excitement. From our window we could see the cathedral of Zagorsk, its blue-and-gold domes like sky and sun. As we traveled along, I saw that even the smallest village had its domed church, but the churches appeared to be deserted, with a lonely look to them.

Dr. Glebov was making the trip into a lesson for the boys. He had stories for each town. When we got to Aleksandrov, the old capital of Russia, where Ivan the Terrible had once ruled, the doctor told us of Ivan's cruel dungeons and tortures.

"He set his hungry bears on anyone he didn't like." Dr. Glebov sighed. "Nothing changes." In a very quiet voice he added, "Now Ivan has come back to us, and this time he rules from Moscow."

It was almost dark when we passed over the bridge across the Volga River. "Mother Volga flows for nearly four thousand miles, boys," he said. "If you got into a little boat here and kept going, you would end up in the Caspian Sea."

From the windows we watched green fields turned into forests and back into fields and meadows. There seemed to be no end to Russia. When I saw there was enough land for everyone in the country to become lost in, I began to understand that there would be no sidewalk or perhaps even no path for Georgi and me along the Yenisey River. I guessed our journey would be a hard one, maybe an impossible one. I wondered if I had been wrong to take Georgi with me. As bad as an orphanage might be, Georgi would have been safe there. If I perished on the journey, Georgi would perish with me. Mama had told me to take care of Georgi. Instead, here we were on our way to great danger, all of my own doing.

Late in the day the train reached the foothills of the Ural Mountains. I knew from my geography books that on one side of the Urals, Russia is more European, and on the other side of the Urals, more Asian. Many people said it was the Asian side that was the real Russia. It was nearly midnight but still light when we reached the eastern side. Dr. Glebov had kept us up, and now he gathered us all at the windows.

"Keep a sharp lookout," he ordered. "There! There! Do you see that white pillar? It is the obelisk that marks where Europe ends and Asia begins. It is something to have seen that."

When we awoke in the morning, we were traveling through the steppes, miles and miles of swamp and meadow dotted with ponds and rivulets. Every now and then a flight of thousands of ducks rose up at the sound of the train, to settle again farther on as if they were playing some game with the train. In the distance the white trunks of the birch trees slashed the blue horizon. While we traveled, we had passed from May to June. In spite of the bits of coal soot from the engine we opened the train windows, and fresh warm breezes blew away the stale air of our compartment. I stuck my head out of the window and felt the wind catch my hair and whip it against my face. We were in Siberia now, and the same wind was blowing over the land where Papa and Mama were.

It was nearly evening of our third day when we crossed the great bridge over the Ob River and reached the outskirts of Novosibirsk, where the

Glebovs were to leave us. I had tried to ready myself
for our farewells. I was resolved not to cry, but inside
I felt I could hardly bear to see them get off the train
and leave us behind.

They had packed their bags and we were saying
our farewells when I noticed Georgi had packed his
own bag.

"No, Georgi," I said. "We stay on the train."

Georgi insisted, "I want to go with Yuri and
Nikolai."

Dr. Glebov was silent for a moment. He gave us a
long look and then said, "Marya, you and Georgi are
welcome to join us. I don't know what our accommo-
dations will be, or what our future can bring, but
surely coming with us will be better than making such
a long journey by yourselves and not knowing whether
at the end of the journey you will find your mother."

But still I could not entirely trust Dr. Glebov, nor
would I give up the idea of finding Mama. I shook my
head.

When the doctor saw that I would not come with them, he sighed but said nothing more. At the moment for parting we threw our arms around one another, blessed one another, and then said good-bye.

Strangers crowded into our compartment to take the Glebovs' place and, seeing Georgi crying, gave me suspicious looks, as if I might have been beating him.

That night was very lonely. Georgi leaned against me, humming quietly to himself. Neither of us slept for more than a few minutes at a time.

The next morning we crossed the Yenisey River. I gave a little gasp. In my mind I had pictured the Yenisey River as a friendly stream that Georgi and I might walk along. There would be meadows with flowers and little houses with friendly people who might take us in and feed us and then send us again on our way. This river looked to be a mile wide. The brown water gushed under the railway bridge and hurried northward as if it were being chased. How could we become friends with such a flood? Were we to travel a thousand miles beside that raging water?

My hand trembled as I gave Georgi his suitcase and took up my own. When we had begun our journey, the train was strange and unfamiliar, an iron monster. Now I longed to let it carry us wherever it wished—anything but to have to leave it for that great sweep of water. It was not a stream that would tag along like a friendly puppy but a torrent that would nip at our heels and chase us on our way like a snarling dog.

CHAPTER SEVEN

PRISONERS

Georgi and I left the train at the Krasnoyarsk station and wandered into the busy city. I knew that I must make some preparations for our trip, but I didn't know where to start. I also knew that I must make our handful of rubles last for three months. As we wandered along, I saw that Georgi was struggling with his suitcase. We could not walk across Siberia carrying suitcases. When I found a secondhand store, I went inside and put our two cases on the counter.

"How much will you give me for these?" I asked the woman behind the counter. She was a short, plump woman nearly hidden by the counter's jumble of plates and pots.

"Where did you steal those suitcases?" She looked suspiciously at the good leather cases, which Mama and Papa had managed to hang on to from the days long ago when their families were wealthy. When she opened the cases and saw our clothes, the package of fruit and bit of ham that was left, and our blankets, her expression changed from suspicion to curiosity.

"Why are you two running away?" she asked. "Have you done something bad?"

I shook my head. Before I could stop him, Georgi said, "We're looking for our mama. The policemen have taken her away."

At once she guessed the truth. "Hush," she said. Though the store was empty, she looked nervously about. "It is a terrible thing when parents are wrenched away from their children and sent off to Lord knows where." She burrowed among the jumbles and drew out two knapsacks. "Put what you must carry in here," she said. "Your suitcases are fine leather. I'll have no trouble getting rid of them." She handed me a little pile of rubles. There was a sad look on her face, as if she were made unhappy by the stories of all the abandoned wares piled up in her store. Now our own story would be an added burden.

I stuffed our belongings into the knapsacks, then put the lighter one on Georgi's back and the larger one on my own.

While the shopkeeper and I transacted our business, Georgi was looking longingly at a small glass globe enclosing a tiny cottage. When he shook the globe, a shower of snow covered the cottage. He watched me put the rubles in my pocket.

"Marya, remember at Christmas there were no presents? Couldn't I have the little cottage in the glass?"

I looked at the price marked on the globe. "It's too much money, Georgi. We need every kopeck." We were nearly at the door when the shopkeeper called Georgi back.

"Here, young fellow, take it." She handed Georgi the globe, and he danced out of the store. I thought that she would make a great deal more on the suitcases than she gave to us, so her giving the globe to Georgi was not terribly generous. Then I was angry with myself for being suspicious.

After peering in the windows of several food shops, I chose the one where the prices were the most reasonable and the flies the least numerous. The June day was warm, and I knew warmer days were ahead. Whatever I chose would have to withstand the heat. I bought dried fruit and dried meat, a large loaf of bread, and a big hunk of hard cheese. I also bought a knife and some matches, for I hoped to hunt small wild animals and cook them over a fire.

With our purchases made and the remaining rubles tied up in a handkerchief and tucked into my pocket, there was nothing to do but to find the river and begin our trip.

Taking Georgi's hand, I walked through the town,

using as our guide to find the river an immense bridge I could see in the distance. When we finally reached the river, I looked longingly at the landing where a steamship was tied up. A line of passengers was filing onto the ship. I saw that each passenger was handing a soldier a little booklet to be stamped. Passports. Even if we had had enough money for tickets, we had no passports and no Dr. Glebov to take us aboard the steamship with his family.

"Marya," Georgi begged, "can't we sit down for a bit? I'm tired, and the straps from the knapsack hurt my back."

I led him along the bank of the river to a grassy spot and was as glad as Georgi to settle down. I knew that we ought to begin our trip, but I didn't know how to take the first step. I tried to study the map I had torn out of my schoolbook, but I had trouble concentrating, for the late-morning sun was pleasant on my back, the grass soft under me, and the June breezes gentle.

The river was crowded with barges and fishing

boats. One of the fishing boats made its way onshore. An elderly man tied up the boat and, slinging a wriggling bag over his shoulder, stepped onto land. He looked about until he saw us.

"You, there," he called. "Come here." He was a wiry man, thin as a birch sapling, with long, wispy white hair. His tanned face was pleated with wrinkles. Though I could think of nothing wrong we had done, he was scowling at us.

Holding hands, we made our way slowly down the bank toward the river.

"Come along," he called out. "I've no time to waste. I must sell these chickens and buy supplies so that I can be in my village by tomorrow night. Nothing is safe in this cursed city. If you two watch my boat for me, I'll give you some kopecks."

He left us with the boat and began climbing up the bank.

"What is the name of your village?" I asked.

He called the name over his shoulder, adding,

"And a poor excuse for a village it is." It seemed he did not like his village any more than the city. As soon as he was out of sight, I got out my map. His village was nearly a hundred miles downstream. A hundred miles was a week's walk. I made up my mind that we would go with him. How much better it would be to float along in a boat than to make our way by foot.

The boat was a long wooden affair, narrow at both ends so that it would skim through the water. I had seen such boats before. Papa and I had often watched the fishermen on the Neva pull into Leningrad to sell their catches. A fishing pole and a landing net were stowed on the bottom of the boat along with a pail, which must have held the bait. Georgi and I would easily fit into the boat.

"Georgi, listen to me. Remember when you were in the play in school and you took the part of the good factory worker who had made more steering wheels for automobiles than anyone else?"

"Yes, and Lev Markovich didn't meet his goal and

the teacher said that made Comrade Stalin very sad, but I made him happy."

"Never mind how happy or sad Comrade Stalin was. You memorized lines for the play."

The corners of Georgi's mouth turned down and his eyes were watery. "Mama helped me."

"Georgi, you must learn some lines now, and I'll help you."

"I don't want to."

"They're very easy—only a few words—and Georgi, if you don't do it right, we will have to walk a hundred miles instead of riding in the boat."

Georgi stood looking at the boat. I could see he was thinking a ride in such a boat would be pleasant.

In a half hour's time the man returned with an armful of supplies, which he began to stow in the boat. He handed each of us five miserly kopecks.

"You can be on your way now," he ordered. "That's all you're going to get."

I took a deep breath. "Please, sir, we are going to

the next village on the river from your own. I'll give you two rubles if you take us along in your boat."

"What? Two children wandering about on their own? You, boy, tell me the truth. What are you doing here?"

Georgi, looking longingly at the boat, recited, "My papa died fighting for the revolution and my mama is sick, and we are to go to my grandmother, who will take care of us."

I sighed with relief. Georgi had not missed a word.

"Two rubles are not enough," the man said.

I had taken two rubles from the little store in my pocket and had them clutched in my hand. I opened my hand and showed them to the man. "It's all I have," I said.

"What's in there?" He gave our knapsacks a greedy look.

"Only our clothes," I answered. He looked at us as if we were two fish at the end of his line, fish he meant to reel in. I began to think we would be foolish to go with him, but I could not find enough courage to begin our long walk.

"All right. Get in," he ordered. "And no scrambling about. You must sit quietly."

We climbed into the boat, Georgi eagerly; but I was still uncertain.

"Watch out there!" he shouted at Georgi. "Do you want to tip us over?"

In a moment we were afloat. The boat was small and the river wide and deep, so we were swept along like a leaf. I forgot my fear, thinking only that we had made a beginning, and when we came to the end of the river, we would find Mama.

When we were safely out into the middle of the river, he asked our names and told us his own.

"I am Yevgeny Vasilievich Savoff, but they call me Old Savoff, though that can be nothing to the two of you."

After that he launched into one vexation after another, making me think he had taken us not for the rubles but to have someone to hear his complaints. The current was strong, and the man did not have to work very hard at his oars, so he had plenty of time for the complaining.

"The streets of the city are filthy and the people are rude and push you about," he said, "and the shop-keepers never lose a chance to cheat you."

I thought of the shopkeeper who had given Georgi the globe, but I made no sound because I could see Old Savoff took pleasure in his grievances and would not be robbed of them. He soon started on us.

"Don't think you will have a long sleep in the morning," he warned. "I must get back to see if that old woman, Fenya, who I was stupid enough to marry, and my useless stepson, Vadim, will have robbed me while I was gone. Every morning Vadim has a sour face when he sees that I am still among the living. He can't wait until he can get his hands on my property. I'll show him. One of these days I'll have my revenge. I'll kick him out of the house, and he will find what it means to work for his bread."

We left the city behind. Overhead the sky was a blue bowl, kingfishers flew among the trees, fishing boats and barges came and went. On the banks of the river were vast green meadows. I felt as if we had been placed in the middle of one of Igor's pretty paintings, yet Old Savoff had not a word to say about the beauty of the June day.

When a bright-blue dragonfly settled on the boat, he swiped angrily at it. When I pointed to a hawk sitting majestically on a pine tree, he growled, "If I had a gun, I would soon make an end of it. Those hawks get after my chickens."

One of the fishing boats was unlike the others. It was large enough for only one person. The fisherman was also unlike the others. I knew from my schoolbooks of the Samoyeds, natives of Siberia who wandered through the Siberian countryside herding reindeer and living off the land. Comrade Tikonov had told us such people were enemies of Russia because they would not obey the orders of the Communist Party to give up their herds of reindeer and live in villages.

The Samoyed in the boat had eyes that tilted down and a face as round and wrinkled as an old apple. His boat skimmed along over the water, and as it passed us, the man raised his paddle in greeting.

Old Savoff grunted. "Why should those people be above the government? They are an ignorant tribe who live in tents instead of houses like civilized people."

"Do they live near here?" I asked.

"Only in the winter. This time of year they gather their herds of reindeer and take them north. I can tell you, when one of their reindeer wanders my way, you can be sure I make a meal of it."

In the middle of the afternoon Old Savoff reached into one of his bags and took out a roll and a chicken leg. Georgi and I watched hungrily as he gnawed away. When he had cleaned the bone, he opened a bottle of beer and drank it in two long drafts.

"No doubt you have your own food," he said.

I took some bread and cheese from my knapsack and shared them with Georgi. We washed them down with handfuls of water from the river.

As the hours passed, I kept thinking Old Savoff would tire, but he kept on with the oars, grumbling all the while, so that I decided that his strength must come from his anger. As long as he kept up his angry complaining, he could keep rowing.

Since it was June and we were in the far north, the sky would remain light all night, but early in the pale light of the evening Old Savoff guided the boat to the shore. He quickly baited his line and cast it out onto the river. In a second the pole bent and he was pulling in a fish. While the fish roasted over a fire, he looked hungrily at our knapsacks.

"What have you got in there?" he asked.

"Just our clothes and a bit of food," I said.

He poked about among my things. "Well, I have

provided the fish," he said. "You can share your bread and cheese."

As I watched him pare a large hunk off the cheese, I said, "I want to take some of that to my grandmother."

He gave me a shrewd look. "I don't believe in your grandmother. What would a *malshyka* like you be doing on your own? It can only be mischief. You are running away. You are lucky I didn't turn you in. When we get to my village, you can make yourself useful around the house."

For a moment I thought of telling him our story as I had told the Glebovs, but such a man was not to be trusted. Old Savoff—with his spite and his grudges, his growling and his talk of revenge—made me think that even a walk of a hundred miles would be better than another hour with such a man.

Old Savoff had rowed all day. Surely he would fall asleep soon. Then, I thought, Georgi and I might steal away in the long white night. By the time he awoke, we would be miles away. We had only to follow the river so that we would not lose our way. While I was making my plans, Old Savoff was watching me.

"I'm turning in now," he said. I was thinking with relief how we would soon be off, when he added with a sly smile, "I have no pillow, so I'll just take one of your knapsacks to ease my head. The other one will cushion my arm." Before I could reach for them, he snatched the two knapsacks and lay down with his arm around Georgi's knapsack and his head on mine. In a moment he was asleep.

I couldn't keep my worry to myself. "Georgi," I whispered, "I think we have to run away from that man, but we can't leave without my knapsack."

"Or mine."

Georgi was not as troubled as I was, for in no time he was asleep, but I lay there watching Old Savoff as he turned and twisted. He grumbled even in his sleep, as if his dreams held further reasons for complaint. It was long past midnight when he shifted his body and his head eased onto the ground, freeing my knapsack. His arm was still tangled in the straps of Georgi's knapsack. I decided we could leave without it. Because Georgi was small, I had carried nearly everything. Georgi's knapsack held nothing but his globe and a few clothes he could do without. Hastily I snatched my knapsack and shook Georgi awake, putting my hand over his mouth so that he would be quiet.

"We are leaving at once."

He sat up, still groggy, and looked about. When he spied his knapsack still wrapped around Old Savoff's arm, tears came into his eyes and his lower lip stuck out. He shook his head.

"No," he said. "I won't leave my little cottage with the snow."

In a whisper I begged, "Georgi, the man is evil and means us no good. We have to escape, and this is our only chance. Tomorrow we will be prisoners in his house."

Georgi put his hands over his ears.

I took his hands away and in an angry whisper I threatened, "If you don't come with me, I'll leave you." With that I got up, swung my knapsack onto my back, and began to walk away.

I went a short distance and looked around quickly to see if Georgi was following me. He was sitting where I had left him, his face scrunched up, tears streaming down his cheeks. He had not moved an inch.

After that I returned and settled hopelessly beside Georgi, who soon fell asleep. I stayed awake for a long while, but Georgi's knapsack stayed where it was. At last I closed my eyes.

I was dreaming that Old Savoff had a whale on the end of his fishing line and would not let it go, making our little boat capsize. I awoke to find Old Savoff shaking me.

"It's five o'clock already," he said in an impatient voice. "Are you going to lie there sleeping all day?"

After a mouthful of bread and cheese we were on

our way. Almost at once the bank, which had been a grassy field, became stone and then rock and steep cliff. Through the sun had come out and the day was warm, I shivered. Suppose we had run away in the night? We would soon have come to the rocks and cliffs. How would we have scrambled over them? We would have had to return to Old Savoff or perish. And what would he have said if he had found us gone only to have us return?

The cliffs turned into rocks and then once again into fields. We passed small villages with their wooden houses and always a deserted church. The villages were inviting, but our boat was in the middle of the river, so there was no escape. Georgi busied himself with watching the flocks of migrating ducks and geese that settled on the river in a rush of flapping and then were off again in feathery arrowheads pointed north.

Old Savoff shook his fist at the flocks of geese. "They'll try to gobble up our seed corn and eat the new wheat, but my rifle will be too much for them.

Last fall when they passed our way, I put an end to half a hundred. We'll have as many geese on our table as we can eat."

I was very hungry, and the thought of a roast goose was pleasant, but I only wanted one goose, not fifty.

The air was filled with birds flying north, tiny brown warblers with patches of yellow, eagles and hawks, and brightly colored birds I had never seen before. I sighed as I thought how in only a few days the birds would be with Mama, while as long as we were in the hands of Old Savoff, we might never see her.

Just then a barge passed us heading north. It was unlike the other barges, with their loads of supplies for the northern cities. This barge was built to hold people. The decks were crowded with men and women—there must have been a couple of hundred packed together. At first I thought the barge a passenger boat, like the steamships, but when I looked more closely, I saw that the people were surrounded by soldiers with guns, and the guns were pointed at the people. The barge passed close enough for me to see the miserable men and women.

I turned to Old Savoff. "Who are they?" I whispered.

"They are prisoners being shipped to the camps in Noril'sk and Dudinka. Stalin knows how to handle people who are enemies of the revolution. The ones who don't starve in the camps will freeze, and it serves them right."

I cried out, "That's a terrible thing to say. How do you know those people aren't innocent?" All I could think of was Mama and Papa.

Georgi was as angry as I was. He kicked at Old Savoff and would have bitten him if I hadn't pulled him away.

Old Savoff gave us a shrewd look. "So that's how it is. You are running away because your parents were arrested. No doubt the authorities would like a word with you."

The sight of the prisoners and the sound of the

word *authorities* so frightened me, I couldn't say a word. After that Georgi and I were very quiet, and Old Savoff kept looking at us as if we were two chickens he was fattening for the pot.

It was early evening when Old Savoff began to pull the boat toward shore and a small cluster of wooden buildings. A young man stood on the bank, his hands on his hips. He was short and stocky, with black hair cut in the shape of an upside-down bowl. His eyes were nearly hidden under bushy brows. The corners of his mouth were turned down. He appeared unhappy to see Old Savoff. He called out, and a woman came running out of the hut wiping her hands on her apron. She was thin and worn like a handkerchief that has been washed until it is threadbare. I thought it must be Fenya, and the young man the stepson, Vadim.

Old Savoff shouted, "Vadim, you lazy dog, why are you standing there? Get the rope to tie the boat. Fenya, you better have something hot on the table or you'll be sorry."

After a surprised look at us, the woman hurried back into the hut. The stepson, walking with deliberate slowness, picked up a coil of rope and sauntered down to the landing. All the while the boat was being made secure with rope, Old Savoff shouted at Vadim.

"After all this time you have no more idea than a dog of tying a proper knot," he scolded. "Do you want the boat to drift off? If I find the plowing has been left for me to do, I'll turn you inside out."

Vadim paid no attention to the threats but stared at Georgi and me.

Old Savoff gave a nasty laugh. "See what I've brought you? A little brother and sister to keep you company. They'll show you what work is. When the boy gets a little older, I'll have no need for your help."

Vadim gave us a hateful look.

We were herded toward the hut, where Fenya was hastily ladling out soup. I saw with relief that places had been set for us. Hungrily we spooned up the soup. Old Savoff was so busy eating, he had no time for complaints. The soup, a fish stew with onions and potatoes and a kind of mushroom I had never tasted, was the best I had ever had.

Fenya hardly took the time to sit down but hovered over us like a mother hen, filling our bowls and cutting more bread when it was needed. I saw that her fine cooking had its purpose, for all the while he was eating, Old Savoff was silent. The moment he came to the end of his food, the grumbling began again.

"Well, Fenya," he said with a wicked smile, "no more excuses about not doing your share of work in the field because you must keep house. Here is a housekeeper for you. She will wash tonight's dishes and sweep up the house. You can go with Vadim to the woods and help him load the firewood. I'll stay and keep an eye on our guests."

He turned to Georgi. "You, boy, don't think you can sit and do nothing. I'll give you a fishing pole. If you don't catch fish, you won't eat." With that he took Georgi to the landing.

There was no water in the house for dishwashing,

so first I had to fill two pails from the river. I found Georgi sitting with his fishing pole in his hand.

In a proud voice he said, "Old Savoff showed me how to put the worms on the hook, and I don't mind anymore if they wriggle a lot and feel slimy."

It was late in the evening by the time I had finished the dishes, swept out the hut, and brought in wood to feed the stove for our breakfast. Georgi was still sitting at the landing. When I went down to see him, I found him in tears.

"My arm is tired and I've used up all the worms and I didn't get any fish."

"Georgi," I pleaded, "come into the house. It's late, and you'll get fish tomorrow."

He wouldn't move. "No. Old Savoff will beat me."

Nothing I could say would make him leave the fishing pole and come with me. I went to meet Fenya, who was returning from the woods, thinking she could help me convince Georgi to come to bed.

"Poor boy," she said. She looked over her shoulder. "Let's hurry and talk with the child before Old Savoff comes."

Georgi was slumped over, fast asleep. The fishing pole had slipped from his hand and fallen into the water. Luckily it had not floated away but was caught in a little clump of reeds.

We heard Old Savoff running toward us. He pushed us aside. "Wake up, you lazy fellow. Just see what you did." He was shaking Georgi. "You get in that river and get my pole. Quick now."

"He can't swim," I pleaded. The current was fast and the river deep. I waded into the water, wondering how I would get to the pole without drowning, for I couldn't swim either. Someone pushed me roughly aside. It was Fenya. In a moment she was swimming toward the reeds as smoothly as an otter. She grasped the pole and swam back, scrambling onto the bank. Shaking the water from her clothes like a dog, she handed the pole to Old Savoff and, picking up

Georgi, headed for the house.

In no time she had changed her clothes and was laying two quilts on the kitchen floor, putting a protesting Georgi to bed. "Not another word," she hushed him. "Marya, you go to bed as well."

Gratefully I sank down on the other quilt, and in seconds I was fast asleep. The last thing I heard was Old Savoff scolding Fenya.

Early in the morning his boot prodded me awake. "Make our breakfast, girl. We should have been in the fields long since."

In spite of Old Savoff's protests, Fenya helped me with the fire when it would not start and reminded me to stir the kasha to keep it from burning.

We all ate standing up. When Vadim tried to pull a chair up to the table, Old Savoff snatched it out of his hand.

"If you had your way, you would lounge about all day and leave the work to me and your mother."

I meant to escape with Georgi the moment they

were off to the fields, but Old Savoff was too smart for me.

"The two of you can come as well," he ordered.

On the way to the fields I whispered to Fenya, "I thought all the farms had been taken over by the state."

Fenya shrugged. "Old Savoff pays off the Party chief in the next village to forget about our farm. Anyhow the state doesn't bother us much here. They think Siberia is only a place to send prisoners." She gave me a long look and I wanted to tell her our story, for I felt she was kind, but Vadim was listening to us and I didn't trust him.

Our first task was to spread manure over the field.

"Take off your shoes to save them," Fenya said. Barefoot, with the muck oozing between our toes, we spread the manure with pitchforks. When the manure was spread, Old Savoff attached the plow to Vadim's back, and the plowing began with grunts and groans from Vadim and cries of "Can't you move a little faster?" from Old Savoff. I was sure that if he'd had a whip, he would have used it on Vadim.

Fenya and I walked along the furrows, carefully placing the seed corn, three to a hill.

Old Savoff kept an eye on us. "Fenya, you will ruin me. You are putting the seeds too close together. Girl, watch yourself. You dropped a seed."

Georgi was put to work chasing the crows that had spied the seed corn and were settling down on the fields with hoarse barkings and coughings. Georgi laughed as he ran at one flock and then another. He flapped his arms and shouted to the crows to leave the seed be.

At noon we ate bread and cheese while Old Savoff told us what a poor job we had done. Though he scolded Fenya as much as he did the rest of us, I saw that she paid him no attention. His angry words were like so many drops of rain slipping away on a window. She must have some power over him, I thought. I began to wonder if so miserable a man could still have room in so sour and shrunken a heart for a crumb of love.

It was early evening before we returned to the cabin for our supper. I could hardly stay awake. My hands were blistered, my back ached, and my face burned from the sun. While I helped Fenya with the dishes, Vadim and Old Savoff walked about outside, talking in low tones. From time to time they looked our way.

Fenya watched them, a worried expression on her face. Finally she said, "They mean you and the boy no good."

I was too tired to care. I didn't see what more they could do to us. We could work no harder than we had, and we could not be more miserable than we were. I thought we would never find Mama. Georgi must have sensed my discouragement, for he fell asleep hanging on to my dress.

It seemed as if I had been asleep only a moment or two when someone shook me. I thought it was Old

Savoff and did not know how I could move, much less go out into the fields again.

I opened my eyes to find Fenya bending over me. "Get up quickly," she said. "They have taken off, and you don't have much time."

Still half asleep, I tried to understand what she was telling me.

"Get up," she repeated. "Old Savoff and Vadim are on their way to the village to see the Communist Party chief. They have guessed your parents have been arrested. We see a lot of that here. They are anxious to get on his good side by turning you in."

"What will they do to us if they catch us?"

"They will send you to one of the prison camps and Georgi to an orphanage."

At the sound of his name Georgi awoke, just in time to hear the word *orphanage*.

"Don't worry," Fenya told him. "Your sister will watch over you."

Her words reminded me of my mother's charge to

care for Georgi, and I could not keep tears from my eyes. Throwing on my clothes, I asked Fenya, "Won't Old Savoff be very angry with you?"

She shrugged. "I can handle the old man. He needs me more than I need him. But where will you go when you leave here? You can't wander about Siberia."

At that I told her our story, but I did not trust her enough to tell her we were going to walk a thousand miles. Instead, I named a village two hundred miles north, for I was beginning to believe our journey might take years, not months.

She shook her head. "Two hundred miles! That's a long way."

"We have the whole summer." What would she say if she knew the truth?

When we were ready to go, Fenya stuffed our knapsacks with bread, cheese, hard-boiled eggs, and dried apples. "Here," she said, handing us a bag of bones. "This is not for you but for the dogs of the village."

It was early morning when Fenya led us outside. She smoothed over a piece of earth and drew a picture with a sharp stick. "Just here the road leaves the river, for the riverbank is nothing but swamp. Then here the road leads to the village where Old Savoff and Vadim have gone. You must stay clear of that village."

She took up the fishing pole that was propped against the hut. "You can't carry a pole through the woods, but take the line. A branch will make a pole, and I'll give you some hooks. You can find bait under any log." She patted Georgi's head. "You will see, you will become a fisherman and the river will feed you."

We both hugged her and clung to her until she pried us loose and sent us on our way. When we looked back, she was wiping away her tears with her apron.

CHAPTER EIGHT

THE RIVER

It was midday when we came to the swamp where the road left the river.

"Look, Marya!" Georgi turned an excited face to mine.

The puddles and pools of the swamp were crowded with birds. There among the reeds and rushes were ducks with brilliant green feathers and ducks with red crests and ducks as black and white as a printed piece of paper. There were geese and long-legged cranes, and here and there stately swans with arched necks. It was as if all the cages in the world had been opened. As soon as one flight of birds landed, another took off. The geese were busy cropping the new grasses while the ducks turned tail up to search the ponds for fish. I would have given anything for the paints I'd had to leave behind.

Georgi and I stood still, holding hands as if we were afraid that in all that soaring, one or the other of us might find ourselves in the sky with the birds. At last we left the swamp to follow the road to the village. The road led though a dark forest filled with cedar trees and another kind of tree whose name I didn't know but whose needles were soft as feathers. At each turn I was afraid we would bump into Old Savoff and Vadim, but we had the road to ourselves. When we heard the dogs bark, we knew we were near the village.

In the distance we could see a row of isbas, the little wooden houses of Siberia. "Hurry," I urged Georgi, pulling him along. "We have to get by the village quickly before Old Savoff sees us."

We had passed the road that led into the village,

and I thought we were safe, when a pack of snarling dogs came after us. In the distance a man looked curiously in our direction.

We were surrounded by the dogs. They were ragged, half-starved beasts that looked like anything would do for a meal, including us. Georgi clung to me. I was sure the villagers would hear the commotion and investigate. Hastily I emptied the bag of bones, scattering them on the ground. While the dogs lunged at them, we made our escape.

The road began to climb. Georgi begged, "Marya, I'm tired. Let's stop and rest."

"We can't, Georgi. We have to get as far from the village as we can. Besides, if we don't walk fifteen miles each day, we won't reach Mama until after the winter starts and we'll freeze to death."

The idea of freezing to death did not quiet him for long. "I don't care if I freeze to death. You can just melt me when the summer comes."

"Don't joke about something so serious, Georgi."

I tried again to tell him how cold it would be when summer ended. When I saw he wouldn't listen, I said, "Georgi, you know all the famous explorers Papa taught us about? Genghis Khan and Marco Polo and Christopher Columbus and all the rest?"

Georgi nodded his head, more interested in the explorers than in talk of his freezing to death.

"Remember, Georgi, what hardships they had? Did they complain?"

Georgi shook his head.

"Well, we are explorers. We will have all kinds of stories of our adventures to tell Mama when we see her."

Georgi looked at me from the corner of his eye. He half believed that we were to be explorers and he half believed I was telling him a tale. At last the wish to be an explorer won, and he trudged after me, complaining about his knapsack and the little black flies, so small you did not know they were there until they bit you. The only comfort we had was the company of the river, which by now was an old friend, tagging along with us wherever we went. The ribbon of water was the color of strong tea and sometimes so wide you could hardly see across it.

When fishermen or barges passed, we were careful to hide behind the trees. When we could walk no longer, we settled down on a sandy bank. I snapped off a branch and fashioned a fishing pole. Georgi eagerly turned over logs and stones and at last held up two fat worms. I was about to fasten them to the hook, but Georgi took the pole from me.

"No. I do the fishing." Much to my horror, he bit one of the worms in half and threaded one half onto the hook.

"Georgi! That's disgusting!"

Seeing how upset I was, he looked very pleased with himself. "Old Savoff taught me how to do that."

This time Georgi was successful, though the two trout he caught were small. He could hardly bear to part with his fish. While he danced around holding a wriggling fish in each hand, I gathered an armful of twigs for a fire. I knew that the trout must be cleaned, but how that was done I had no idea. In the city the few fish we could buy were ready for the pan.

"You have to get to their insides and take them out," Georgi said. "Only I think you should kill them first."

We whopped the fish against a stone, and I made a long cut in each one's belly. Gritting my teeth, I reached into the fish and pulled out whatever would come out. I whittled points on two green branches and stuck the fish on the points, and Georgi and I held the branches over the fire.

The fish were very tasty and the fire cheerful. I began to think that the journey would be possible after all. I fell asleep at once, only to be awakened by Georgi shaking me.

"There's something there," he whispered.

I thought of the great Siberian mammoth Papa had showed us in the Leningrad museum. Might there be such animals still on the earth? Then I remembered that mammoths ate buttercups, and I felt better.

There were scampering, rustling sounds and then nothing. It must have been after midnight, though it was light as day out. I sat up and looked around, but there was nothing to see. I didn't have the courage to climb out of my blanket. It was a long time before we fell asleep again, and then we woke at every noise. In the morning we found tracks circling the place where I had left the fish's insides. The prints were small, so the animal was not worth worrying about.

After a quick breakfast of bread and cheese, and a reminder to Georgi that we were explorers who did not complain, we started out. I had no idea how much ground we were covering, but I thought if we walked for two hours in the morning, two hours in the afternoon, and two hours in the early evening, we would have walked fifteen miles a day. Since Old Savoff's boat had already carried us a hundred miles, by the summer's end we should have traveled the thousand miles to Dudinka and our mother.

The first three days went very well. The path followed along the river, so we had the river's company, water to drink, water to bathe our feet, and ducks, boats, and barges to watch. We saw no more barges carrying prisoners.

On the other side of the path was a forest, a little too dark and too crowded with huge trees to be a friend. Sometimes we sensed movement in the woods, so we knew we had invisible animals for company, but they kept to themselves. Once, when the trees gave way to a meadow, we found a field of wild strawberries. We spent a whole precious hour on our hands and knees gently twisting the strawberries, like tiny red rubies, from their delicate stems. All the while we picked, beetles and ants climbed over our sticky fingers. At last we fell back onto the ground, our mouths stained red and our bellies full.

By eating mostly fish, we saved what little food we had. Georgi was becoming a good fisherman, even throwing back into the river fish he pronounced too small. After we lost a chunk of bread to a thieving wolverine, we learned to hang our knapsacks from tree branches. Since it never got dark, it was hard to tell when night came and went, but when we were too full of fish and too tired to walk any farther, we rolled up in our blankets and went to sleep until the early-morning birdsong awoke us. Georgi was eagerly playing the part of explorer. He would dash into the woods after "lions" and "tigers," returning minutes later to announce he had frightened away the wild beasts.

At the end of our first week Georgi caught a large fish. While I was cleaning it, Georgi wandered into the woods. I thought nothing of it when he ran out of the woods shouting, "It's a bear and it's got two Russes with it!"

I was sure it was part of his game. "Georgi," I said, "stop running into the woods. No wonder you get so tired. Stay on the path."

"Marya, there's a bear coming!" Georgi grabbed me around the waist and hung on. I could feel his heart pounding against me. I looked up to see a brown bear with two cubs. In that huge body the bear's eyes looked very tiny and very angry. Her lip was drawn, showing her sharp teeth. The bear lumbered toward us. When the cubs followed their mother, she slapped them so that they tumbled onto their backs. I knew what that huge paw, as large as a dinner plate, could do to us. A tree, I thought; but no, bears climbed trees. Run? Bears were fast runners. Then it came to me: the dogs and the bones! I scooped up the fish, tossing it in front of the bear. At my quick movement, the bear rose up on her hind feet. She looked huge. A moment later she was nosing the fish, and then, seated on her rump, she began tearing it apart.

I grabbed Georgi, and we ran along the river path as fast as we could, never looking back. We must have run a half mile when we finally stopped on a hill overlooking the river.

"Let's keep going," Georgi pleaded.

"We can't. We have to go back for our knapsacks." I was panting so hard, I had trouble getting the words out.

"They'll eat us if we go back."

"We must wait until they're gone."

We sat very close together on the hill and looked out at the river. There were no boats or barges to be seen, just the brown river and two ducks looking unprotected as they swam alone on the wide stretch of water. The two ducks suddenly shot up into the air. Downstream the mother bear and the cubs were frolicking in the water, splashing one another. After a few minutes of play the mother and the cubs swam across the river and, climbing out on the other side, loped away.

I am not sure why, but I began to cry. Georgi patted my shoulder. "They've gone away now, Marya. You don't have to be scared."

I knew now how many dangers the woods held. I did not see how we would ever reach Mama. That was not all. Though I couldn't tell Georgi, seeing the mother watching over and playing with her two cubs made me miss Mama more than ever. I was tired of being brave and tired of being in charge. I didn't believe we could make such a long journey. I wanted to lie down in the woods and never get up again.

Georgi was watching me.

"Come on, Marya," he said. "I'll show you the way back to the knapsacks."

I made myself get up and follow him.

We found our knapsacks broken open and our belongings scattered everywhere. Our last bit of food had been eaten. I began to think even an orphanage would have been better than starving in the woods.

The next day there were no bears, but there was rain—not a gentle rain, but a downpour. It felt like someone had turned on a faucet and we were standing under the stream of water. The path turned to mud. Our clothes clung to us as if we had been wrapped in wet sheets.

Georgi said, "Marya, it's raining so hard, I can't keep my eyes open."

We tried to find shelter under the branches of the trees, but the wind blew the rain across us as well as over us. Georgi and I broke off branches from the pine trees, weaving them back and forth among the boughs of a tree until we had a shelter. The drops still found their way to us, but we weren't being drowned anymore.

We sat all day under the tree while I worried that no miles would be covered. When Georgi became restless, I told him Pushkin's story of poor Yevgeny. The great Russian poet Pushkin described how terrible rains came to St. Petersburg until the Neva River burst her banks and flooded the whole city. "Smashing and slaying, destroying and pillaging," Pushkin wrote. When poor Yevgeny found that his sweetheart was drowned, he became a madman, wandering the city day after day and night after night. One night in his misery Yevgeny cursed the great bronze statue of Peter the Great on his horse. The bronze statue came to life and began to ride after Yevgeny, chasing him through the city until the terrified man fell exhausted and died. Georgi loved the story, for Mama had often taken us to see the statue of the bronze horseman.

"It won't rain so hard that the Yenesey will flood like the Neva did?" Georgi asked.

I promised it wouldn't, but it was still raining when evening came. We had no fish and no fire. Curling up on the wet ground on wet blankets, we tried to sleep. Early in the morning the rain turned into a thunderstorm. With the first bolt of lightning I pulled Georgi away from our shelter under the tree and out into the open.

"What are you doing, Marya? You are getting us all wet again."

"We can't sit under the tree, because we might get struck by lightning."

We were standing in a clearing. The pale sky that

never darkened was dark now with storm clouds. The river seethed and roiled.

"If we keep standing here, Marya," Georgi whined, "the lightning will find us." Georgi started back toward the shelter of the tree.

There was a terrible crack, as if the whole world were splitting in two. Only a few feet from us a huge tree branch crashed to the ground. After that we did not dare go into the woods.

As suddenly as it began, the storm ended. In an hour's time a pale morning sun shone, warming the ground so curls of steam rose all around us. We wrung out our clothes and hung them on branches. While we waited for them to dry, we saw a marten poke its head out of a hole in the branch that had split from the tree. It had a baby marten in its mouth. The animal made its way to the ground and then up a nearby tree. It disappeared into a hole and then, without the baby, scampered back to the first hole to collect a second and then a third and a fourth baby to carry back to its new nest. To make its way from its old nest to the new one, the marten had to cross just in front of us. We kept very still. Each time, the marten paused, looked our way, seemed to decide we were not dangerous, and hurried by us.

The marten cheered us. The sun was hot now, and our clothes dried quickly. The river settled down. Georgi caught a large fish with pink flesh that was very tasty. We set out in a good mood, walking most of the day to make up for the day we had lost. After that we made good time each day, and though we never went hungry, we grew very tired of fish twice a day.

We passed two small villages, but I thought in a town where everyone would be known, we would stand out. At last we came to a larger town. We washed well, combed our hair, and cleaned our clothes as best we could, and holding my breath, I took Georgi's hand. We made our way into the town searching for a store where I thought no questions would be asked. We came upon an outdoor market where people appeared to have come from all around the countryside. Georgi and I mixed easily with the crowds. I spent precious kopecks on cheese, bread, and plump raspberries. We hurried away before anyone could ask questions. That evening we had a feast.

Twice we came to large rivers that flowed into the Yenisey. Each time we found a fisherman willing to ferry us across the river for a ruble. "The crossing of the river with this east wind will be hard work," the first fisherman said. "Just see those clouds shaped like a blacksmith's anvil," the second fisherman said. "A storm is on the way."

The fishermen asked no questions of us. They knew that in Siberia everyone had secrets. Only the talk of weather was safe, for the weather had no secrets and was there for everyone to see.

Mosquitoes had been bothering us for days. Though we beat the air around us with a spray of leaves as we walked, our arms and legs were covered with red bumps. On a morning when the air was so still that not a leaf or a blade of grass stirred, the mosquitoes suddenly fell upon us like a plague, biting us everywhere. If we talked, mosquitoes got in our mouths. If we breathed, we breathed in mosquitoes. All the running and slapping and covering of our heads didn't help. We were hurrying down the river path, flailing away with our arms, when Georgi called out, "Look, Marya, there are branches standing still in the river."

While we tried to puzzle out why the branches didn't float with the current, three reindeer heads emerged, dripping water. The reindeer were standing in the river, their branched racks poking out.

For a moment, in the magic of seeing the reindeer, we forgot the mosquitoes. I had learned in school that hundreds of thousands of reindeer roamed the plains of Siberia. Some of them would be gathered together in herds by the Samoyeds. Others, like these, migrated across the land.

"Why are they in the river?" Georgi asked. "Are they fishing?"

I knew that reindeer grazed on mosses and lichen and did not eat fish. As we swatted away the mosquitoes, I suddenly realized what the reindeer were doing in the river. They were escaping the mosquitoes. Minutes later the reindeer lifted their heads to see us slip into the water. Silently they swam away. For a glorious half hour we were free of the mosquitoes. The next morning a wind blew the mosquitoes away.

CHAPTER NINE

CARRIED AWAY

Each day I broke off a bit of twig and put it carefully in my pocket. In that way I kept track of the days. Each evening Georgi would ask for the little pieces and we would count them off. We had twenty-five pieces, but the journey seemed much longer. Each evening Georgi begged, "Marya, turn out your pocket. There have to be more pieces."

With the hundred miles we had gained in Old Savoff's boat, and allowing for days when it rained, I figured we must have traveled nearly five hundred miles, but that was not even halfway.

The river took care of us like a mother. Each day

it fed us fish. It washed us and washed our clothes. It gave us water when we were thirsty. Always it ran ahead of us to show us the way. On the days that the path wandered into the woods and we lost sight of the river, we were sad and troubled. It was like losing Mama all over again.

There were barges and steamboats and the boats of fishermen on the river. Often the river had surprises for us: a busy muskrat or a slinky mink swimming about, and strange, long-legged birds that stalked the shore for frogs. There were huge birds overhead, some with white heads and some with white bellies, that fished the river with their beaks and talons. Often, now, we saw reindeer. I thought how Old Savoff had talked of a roasted reindeer, but I did not see how we were to hunt one and I didn't think I could get one to lie down and be roasted.

I was frightened to discover that the buying of bread and cheese to eat with our fish, and paying for being ferried, had used up all our rubles but one. I resolved not to spend that one, though Georgi begged me for bread, saying without it he would not eat another bite of fish.

"If I get a bone in my throat, Marya, we won't have any bread to get it down and I'll choke to death. Besides, you don't cook the fish enough, and they taste slimy and they smell."

I felt exactly like Georgi about the fish, but I couldn't say so. Because Georgi liked to fish, and because he was hungry, I could still coax him to take a few bites, but it was hard to comfort Georgi when I was so discouraged myself.

It was a morning in July when Georgi said, "Marya, I won't take another step. You said we would see Mama, but we don't see anything but water and trees."

For the thousandth time I took out the map, which was in shreds. Measuring from the last village we had passed, I saw the next village was miles away, much farther than I had thought. Even if we spent our last ruble in that village on food, the food would be gone long before we were anywhere near Dudinka. At the rate we were going, we would walk into winter before we walked into Dudinka.

Always before, I had been able to persuade Georgi. Always before, I had believed in our journey, but Georgi was only saying out loud what I had been thinking for days. I could not see how we could walk hundreds of miles with no food other than bony, slimy, evil-smelling fish. Our shoes were nearly worn though—each morning I had to pack them with grass. Our clothes were ripped and worn. Our faces were burned from the sun and our arms and legs were covered with bites.

Though I thought and thought, I could see no way to keep going. It might be that I could push myself a little farther, but I could not push Georgi. Either we would lie down in the woods and die or we would have to go on to the next village and give ourselves up. If we were lucky, we would be sent to an orphanage.

If we were unlucky, we would end up in a prison camp.

"Georgi, if I let you rest here all day, will you walk to the next village? It's only two or three days away, and I promise we'll spend a whole ruble on food." I did not tell him about the orphanage or the prison camp.

He gave me a suspicious look. "Tell me what food you'll buy, Marya."

"Bread, cheese, raisins, milk, and cake."

"Cake? You promise to buy cake?"

I nodded. If we were going to prison, why shouldn't we have cake first? They would certainly take away any money we had.

"All right," Georgi said.

"But Georgi, we have to eat something until we can get to the village, so you must fish."

I tied the line with its hook onto a branch while Georgi turned over a decaying log and pulled out a large bug with more legs than anything should need.

While Georgi fished, I stuffed my shoes with handfuls of grass. As I was putting them on, I heard a crashing noise, followed by shouts. Two men rushed out of the woods and grabbed Georgi. Before I could reach Georgi, a dozen more men, all Samoyeds like the first two, some perched high on the shoulders of reindeer, came thundering through the woods.

I grabbed Georgi and began a tug-of-war with the Samoyeds. "Let him go!" I shouted. Georgi's eyes were very wide. He was too startled to say a word.

While the men hung on to Georgi, gesturing and shouting angrily in a language I could not understand, a Samoyed jumped off of his reindeer and spoke to me in Russian.

"The boy is fishing in the shaman's own fishing place. It is a holy place, and no one but the shaman can fish there." The other Samoyeds looked very angry, but the one who spoke to us only looked worried.

Still hanging on to Georgi, I pleaded with him. "Make them let go of my brother. We didn't know the place belonged to your whatever-you-call-him. We'll go and fish someplace else."

Georgi was crying. "I don't even like fish," he sobbed. "He can have them all."

The man said Samoyed words to the others, and they let go of Georgi, but still they appeared very angry. More Samoyeds climbed down from their reindeer and gathered around us, shouting and gesturing. They argued with the man who spoke Russian.

"What are they saying?" I asked.

"I have told them to let you go on your way, but they say the shaman must decide if you are to be punished."

One man grabbed me, and another picked up Georgi and our knapsacks. Georgi and I struggled to get away, but the men only laughed at our efforts. In seconds we were lifted onto the backs of reindeer. A man sprang up behind each of us, and we went galloping through the woods.

I was well up on the shoulders of the reindeer. A

bridle was threaded around the animal's antlers, but there was no saddle. I was sure I was going to fall off the galloping beast. I half hoped I would. If I wasn't killed first, I might escape. But what if Georgi did not fall off at the same time? I would never see him again. With one hand I grasped the reindeer's shoulder; with the other I clung to the Samoyed.

We tore though the woods, bumping along and dodging trees while all the while the Samoyeds shouted to one another. Just when I thought all my insides had been jumbled together, I saw a meadow in the distance covered with tents and, beyond the tents, hundreds of reindeer herded together. Samoyed men, women, and children hurried to meet us.

The presence of the children, some of them Georgi's and my ages, made the Samoyeds less threatening. Their clothes were fashioned from hide and trimmed with rows of brightly colored embroidery. The women wore scarfs that covered their long black braids. Standing to one side, a little apart from the rest of the tribe, was a very old man dressed in a long robe of hide painted with a picture of an eagle. The robe was decorated with strips and braids of hide, fringes, tassels, and little bells. On the man's head was a peaked hat with long fringes that hung down over his shoulders.

With much chattering, not a word of which we could make out, Georgi and I were pulled and pushed toward the old man. I was sure he was the man who would decide if we were to be punished. I didn't know how Samoyeds punished people, but I was sure I would not like it.

As Georgi and I stood before him holding hands, the man walked around us, poking us with his finger, exclaiming as if we were haunches of meat he was considering buying. At last he called out, "Edeiko," and the man who spoke Russian ran over to us. Edeiko, for that must have been his name, spoke rapidly, pointing to us from time to time.

At last he turned to us. He was frowning. "The

shaman is very angry with you for fishing in his holy place. Because you are only children, he will let you go, but you must give him a gift to make up for what you have taken from him."

"All we have is this," I said. I put my hand in my pocket and slowly brought out my last ruble. We might have to starve, but at least we would be free.

Edeiko shook his head sadly. "Money would insult the shaman. What do you have in there?" He pointed to our knapsacks.

My heart sank. "Nothing," I answered truthfully. "Only worn-out clothes and our blankets." Having seen the splendidly decorated clothes worn by the Samoyeds, I was sure our rags would be even more insulting to the shaman than a ruble.

The shaman was already exploring the knapsacks, tossing our things out onto the ground, making noises that sounded like disgust. When he came to Georgi's globe, he paused. He carefully took up the globe, turning it this way and that so that the snow fell onto the little cottage. He waited until the snow settled and then shook it again, uttering cries of delight. By now half the village had crowded around the shaman, and all were exclaiming over the globe.

"What are they saying?" I asked Edeiko.

"They say it is very great magic," Edeiko said.

Hardly daring to breathe, I said, "Tell the shaman if he will give us some food and let us go, he can have the globe." We would have our freedom and the ruble as well.

Georgi snatched his hand from mine. "That globe is mine, Marya. You have no right to give it away." Before I could stop him, he ran toward the shaman and grabbed the globe. "It's mine! You can't have it!"

Everyone was silent. There were looks of horror on their faces at Georgi's behavior toward the shaman.

Desperately I turned to Edeiko. "Tell them he is only a little boy and doesn't know what he's doing." But Georgi's fiery behavior must have convinced the shaman that the globe was even more precious than he thought. The shaman spoke to Edeiko.

Edeiko turned to me and said, "The shaman will give you two reindeer for the globe."

We might eat one of the reindeer and harness the other one, riding it to Dudinka, but I could not imagine myself butchering a huge beast whose meat would spoil in a day or two. And how were we to climb up on the back of a strange reindeer and make it go where we wanted?

"Georgi," I pleaded, "you have to let them have the globe or they'll never let us go. I have a ruble. I can buy you another one."

"I don't want another one. I want this one. Anyhow, I don't believe you. You said we were going to find Mama, and where is she?" He hugged the globe to his chest. "They can't have it."

Though he could not understand Georgi's words, the shaman must have known what he meant, for he spoke angrily to Edeiko.

Edeiko gave us a regretful look. "The shaman will not steal the globe, for stealing is forbidden, but you and your brother must travel with us, and your brother must allow the shaman to have the little cottage in his hands from time to time."

I was furious with Georgi and wondered if I might convince the shaman that the globe was really mine and that I would gladly give it to him, but seeing the way Georgi was clutching the globe to his chest, I knew I would not be believed. Even if I were, Georgi would never allow me to give the globe away.

In a hopeless voice I said, "Where is the tribe traveling to?" I saw us wandering forever in Siberia's endless emptiness, each day taking us farther from Mama.

"We are gathering our herds of reindeer. In the winter we travel south with them. As the weather warms, we herd them north to the mouth of the river and the tundra, where they graze on the mosses and the lichen, fattening up for the winter to come."

All I heard was *the mouth of the river*.

Holding my breath, I asked, "Do you go by the town of Dudinka?"

"We don't go near cities, but we will be one or two days' journey from there."

Trying to hide my excitement, I asked, "How long will the journey take?"

"Three or four weeks."

"Can you travel so fast?"

"The reindeer carry us."

I could not believe how lucky we were. In a little over three weeks, traveling with the Samoyeds and fed by them, we would be with Mama. I tried not to show my happiness and my relief. I wanted them to think we were doing them a favor by accompanying them instead of the other way around.

"Please tell the shaman we will go with you and he may have the globe in his hands whenever he pleases."

Georgi began to protest.

"Listen to me, Georgi," I said. "No one is going to

take the globe from you. The shaman only wants to play with it a bit. Mama always taught you to share your toys." I bent over and whispered into his ear, "Georgi, they will take us to Mama in Dudinka, and we'll get there on the backs of the reindeer—no more walking."

Georgi considered all that I had said. I could have shaken him, for I could see he was getting great pleasure from being the center of attention. He meant to enjoy the attention as long as he could. "Georgi." I gave him a little push. At last he nodded. Reluctantly he handed the globe to the shaman.

I believe Edeiko was our friend, for he looked relieved. Quickly he said a few words to the shaman. The shaman nodded his head and gestured toward the Samoyed women. Immediately the women crowded around us, exclaiming over our shoes. Before we could stop them, they toppled us and pulled off our shoes, throwing them away with disgust. One of the women disappeared into a tent. When she came out, she was carrying two pairs of boots like those the Samoyeds wore. Georgi was given a pair to put on. With much shaking of their heads and many scolding noises, they handed me a much taller pair. I had not realized how much I had grown, and the Samoyed women gave me the impression that they considered it unseemly in a woman to show so much of her legs.

The boots were made of the softest reindeer hide, with the fur scraped off. They were covered with embroidery done with brightly colored threads. Edeiko proudly explained that the soles of the boots were made from skins taken from beneath the hooves of the reindeer, so they would wear well. While I squirmed at the thought of the poor reindeer, the boots felt so light, I might have been walking on air.

"They are boots our own children have out-grown," Edeiko said. "But much labor has gone into them, so they are never discarded but kept for the next child who needs them."

I was as pleased with the gift as Georgi, who was

tramping about in his boots, causing much giggling.

After a bit the women went off to prepare dinner. We were left on our own, but we were never out of sight of the shaman. The shaman could not guess the favor he was doing us, and all because Georgi had refused to give up his little cottage in the snow. I reached for Georgi and gave him a hug. He was so startled, his mouth dropped open.

"Why are you crushing me like that, Marya?"

"We mustn't let them know, Georgi, but they'll take us nearly to Mama. Then we can give them the globe." There was a stubborn look on his face. "Georgi, when we're that close to Mama, you'll have to give it up. Otherwise they'll make us go to the Arctic Sea."

"I don't care," Georgi said. "We learned in school there are polar bears in the Arctic Sea. I want to see the polar bears."

"Georgi, what about Mama?"

There were tears in his eyes. "I don't believe Mama

is where you said. I don't think we'll ever see her again." With that he ran off. I was surprised to see him head for the shaman. Together they played with the little cottage, the old man as happy as Georgi with the toy.

The delicious smells of roasting meat coming from a fire pit made me realize how hungry I was. I wandered over to the pit, where a very large part of a reindeer was being turned on a spit. I had never seen so much meat in all of my life. It was all I could do to keep from tearing off a bit of the tasty flesh.

While two women tended the spit, the rest of the women along with three young girls, one my age, set out baskets filled with strange-looking things.

When the women called to the men, the men came with their knives and cut great hunks of meat, which they presented to the shaman, who said some words over the meat and then signaled the men to distribute it.

There were no forks, but Georgi and I hadn't had

forks in weeks. We tore into our portion, chewing the delicious meat until the juices ran down our chins. Baskets were passed about, and the women urged us to eat. In one basket there were little nuts. "Pine nuts," Edeiko explained. Another basket held dried fruit. "Cranberries," he said, "and cloudberries." We helped ourselves from the third basket to something that tasted crisp and crackly as we chewed it. Edeiko said, "Mouse nests."

I gave a little screech. Edeiko smiled. "The women dig them and dry them in the sun. The mice make their nests from the roots of a lily, which is much admired for its tastiness."

When dinner was over, the shaman called Georgi to him. The globe was produced, shaken several times, and then given reluctantly back to Georgi.

"The shaman is going to tell you a story," Edeiko said to Georgi, "and I will translate it for you." Edeiko's voice was very solemn, so we knew that we were honored. All the men and women drew close to the shaman. They looked like little children eager for a bedtime story.

The shaman's voice, which was usually shrill and bossy, became soft and dramatic, as if he were seeing the story unfold before his eyes as he told it.

"Once there was a bear," he said. "The bear was very old and very wise. It was the month when the salmon return to the river. The wise old bear put one of his huge paws into the river to catch a slippery salmon. There were other bears fishing the river, but they respected the old bear and would not move into his territory.

"Among these younger bears was a foolish bear. Though the river was full of salmon for the taking, the younger bear moved into the old bear's territory. He was quicker than the old bear. As the old bear reached for a fish, the younger one would snatch it away. The old bear growled and showed his teeth, but still the young bear snatched the salmon from under the old bear's nose. He believed the old bear was too old and too weak to fight him. As he challenged the old bear, he looked at the other bears to be sure they saw how clever he was and what a fool he was making of the old bear.

"The other bears drew closer. The young and foolish bear thought, *They are coming closer the better to see how clever I am.*

"All at once the other bears attacked the foolish bear, nipping at his ears and swiping at him with their powerful paws. Their claws scratched, and their teeth hurt him. For a moment the foolish bear was too startled to move; then he lumbered hastily away. Later, whining and complaining, he asked of the other bears, 'Why did you attack me? I was doing nothing to harm you.'

"One of the younger bears replied, 'When you make our leader appear weak, we are all in danger.' "

Georgi looked a little puzzled, but there were murmurs of approval from the men and women who had gathered to hear the story.

Suddenly Georgi said, "I have a bear story as well." Edeiko frowned at such boldness, but he translated Georgi's words. The shaman looked surprised but indicated that Georgi should tell his story.

Georgi described the mother bear and her two cubs and how we had escaped by giving them our fish.

The shaman laughed with delight, clapping Georgi on the back, nearly tipping him over. He said some words to Edeiko. Edeiko said, "The shaman wishes the boy to sleep in his tent with him and his wife and children."

I thought Georgi would refuse, not wanting to leave me, but he went happily along with the shaman, only giving me a look that said, "See, I am more important than you are."

A girl my age took me by the hand. "That is Tadibe," Edeiko said. "You will stay with her." Tadibe had a round face with pink cheeks and bright black eyes. Her raven hair hung in two long braids. She was smiling but could not stop staring at me, as if she had been given a curious animal to watch over.

Tadibe led me into one of the tents and gave me a reindeer skin to sleep on. The skin was soft and much more comfortable than the ground and the thin blanket that had been our bed for weeks. Curled up in the tent were Tadibe's parents and her brothers and sisters. As tired as I was, I found it impossible to fall asleep, for Tadibe sat cross-legged, staring at me. Even after the staring stopped and she fell asleep, all the turning and breathing and snuffling that went on around me kept me awake. Though I was sure he was safe with the shaman, I missed Georgi, for I had never before slept with him out of my sight.

A heavy rain began to fall. The drops pelted the tent, making a dancing sound. If we had not been found by the Samoyeds, Georgi and I would be lying wet and hungry in the woods, or worse, separated forever in some orphanage. Here we were sheltered, our stomachs full, even if part of the fullness was the nests of mice. Best of all, we would soon be traveling toward Mama.

The journey north began in the morning. While the men gathered the reindeer herd, the women took down the tents, stacking the tent poles and the rolls of hide that had covered them.

Georgi stayed close to the shaman, whose only task seemed to be to urge everyone to move more quickly. I watched what Tadibe did and tried to do the same, but I stumbled under the weight of the tent poles, which were awkward and too heavy for me. I was a little better at rolling up the hides. When the journey begin, the shaman spent much time deciding which path would be auspicious.

"The spirits of his ancestors guide him," Edeiko explained.

At last one path was chosen. I was surprised to see a woman mounted on a reindeer take her place at the head of the procession.

It was an amazing sight, the woman followed by the shaman and finally the rest of us mounted on reindeer. Trailing the procession were sleighlike carts cleverly fashioned of birch bark and hide. Each cart was drawn by a team of six reindeer. At the very end of the procession came the herders with hundreds of reindeer.

We made few stops, and those only for a moment or two. Food was a handful of dried currants or a twist of dried reindeer meat eaten on the trail.

I was mounted on a reindeer with Tadibe, who was getting used to me now and who chattered on, not caring that I could not understand her. Tadibe took pleasure in everything around her and could not bear to wait until we knew one another's language to share her delight. By the day's end I knew the Samoyed words for *tree*, *water*, *river*, *sun*, *reindeer*, and *sore bottom*, while Tadibe had learned the same words in Russian.

In the evening everything repeated itself backward. The women put up the tents and the men looked after the herd. While Georgi and the shaman were busy with the globe, Tadibe and I joined some of the children gathering wood for the fire. By the time we had accumulated a stack of wood, the men had butchered a reindeer. I followed Tadibe to the animal, which had been skinned and cut into joints. To one side were the reindeer's intestines. I quickly looked away, but when I looked back I was horrified to see Tadibe and several women emptying the contents of the intestines, which were not what I feared they would be but a kind of green mess that looked like half-digested plants. The women added reindeer blood and fat and stirred the mess into a pudding. The loathsome mixture was hung in a skin over the fire to smoke. With much oohing and aahing, the pudding was sliced and handed around along with the meat. Georgi, who had not seen its preparation, took a large slice. He smiled and nodded his head. The shaman looked on approvingly. I said nothing to Georgi, a small revenge for his shameless showing off the day before.

Toward the end of the meal, the shaman called us over and handed Georgi and me each a round black object he had plucked from the edge of the fire. He presented them to us as if they were great delicacies, and I heard all around us little gasps of approval. Georgi popped his into his mouth, chewed, and swallowed, looking only a little puzzled. I did the same. There was not much flavor to the morsel. It was chewy, almost fighting back when I bit on it. At last I got it down.

"What is it?" I asked Tadibe. She guessed what I was asking and pointed first to what was left of the reindeer and then to her eyes. At first I thought she was saying, "Can't you see? It's a part of the beast." But Edeiko, who was watching us, smiled and said, "The shaman has given you the choicest bits, the reindeer's eyeballs. He has bestowed a great honor on you and your brother."

I wanted to throw up, but I managed a sickly smile and kept my mouth tightly shut. Georgi did not mind at all. He grinned and looked around as if he wanted a second helping.

CHAPTER TEN

THE GOVERNMENT MAN

Each day the reindeer took us farther north; each day we were closer to Mama. I had seven new pieces of twig in my pocket and many new words, for Tadibe and I were becoming fast friends, chattering back and forth, first in her language and then in mine. She gave me a fine shift of reindeer hide to replace my worn dress and braided my hair for me. She even gave me a scarf to tie on my head so that I would look like her. We seldom stopped talking, for we were eager to know each other's language so we could learn about each other's worlds.

It was the time of year that the reindeer had their

fawns. Tadibe and I loved to watch the spindly-legged fawns trot after their mothers. When the tribe rested, the fawns would eagerly nurse and then curl up against their mothers and fall asleep.

One night Tadibe nudged me awake, motioning me to follow her out of the tent. The heavens were on fire. Streaks of orange and red raked the sky. The colors played a kind of tag, shifting first here and then there. To keep our heads from snapping off our necks, Tadibe and I lay on the ground, the better to watch. I had heard of the northern lights, and I supposed there was some scientific explanation for them. I liked Tadibe's better. She said the Samoyed word for *embroidery* and pointed to the stripes of colors that flashed across the sky. She was saying that the gods were decorating the sky. I longed for my paints, yet I knew my little daubs of color would be as a few raindrops were to a flood.

We had been with the Samoyeds a week when I awoke in the morning to excited shouts. A moment later Tadibe was shaking me. She called out a single word that I had never heard before. I saw the tent was empty apart from Tadibe and me. I sprang up, pulled on my boots, and ran with Tadibe out of the tent opening.

The moment I stepped outside, I was lost. A fog had crept in from the river and settled like a veil over the land. Everything had disappeared: the tents, Tadibe, and the people whose worried voices I could hear.

"Tadibe," I called, "where are you?" I felt a hand on my arm. She spoke the word for *reindeer*, which I understood, and then in a frightened voice another word that I did not understand until the desperate voices of the men came to me from first one place and then another, close and then far, and then close again, as they were calling the reindeer. Loudest of all the voices was the voice of the shaman, who half shouted, half chanted words that seemed to be at once a desperate plea and an angry scolding. It was as if he were angry at his gods but also begging for their help.

At last I understood. The reindeer were lost in the fog. When I heard Edeiko's voice nearby, I called to him. He had no time for me, merely telling me that the reindeer must be found before they were lost forever.

There was no food that morning, no taking up of tents and riding on. There were only the plaintive calls of the men, often from a great distance as they ran helplessly about in the fog searching for the herd.

Georgi was anxious to follow the men, but much to his disgust I made him stay close to me. I could not bear to think of my brother swallowed up by the thick emptiness of the fog.

It was noon before the fog began to lift. Little bits of our world were given back—a piece of tent, a pair of boots, the trunk of a tree, and at last a scrap of sky.

The men and many of the women were gone. Only the older women and the children remained. As the women and children became visible, I saw the fear on their faces. I knew the survival of the tribe depended on the reindeer. The reindeer gave them food and clothes and the coverings for their tents. I had watched the women sewing with the sinews of the reindeer. The antlers of the reindeer became buttons and handles. The sale of a part of the herd brought the only money the Samoyeds had.

I was so caught up in what was happening, I hardly listened to Georgi, who was mumbling something to me. When I turned to him, I heard him say, "I gave the shaman my globe. Edeiko said the shaman needed it to find the reindeer." There was a worried look on Georgi's face. I thought he was fearful that the globe would be lost. But it wasn't that.

"Marya," he said in a frightened voice, "what if my globe doesn't work?"

Alarmed, I asked, "What do you mean, Georgi?"

"I mean, what if the little cottage doesn't find the reindeer?"

I saw that the shaman's regard for the globe had convinced Georgi that it really had magic powers.

"Georgi, that's nonsense. The shaman only thinks

that because he has never before seen anything like the globe."

Angrily Georgi said, "That's not true! It *is* magic."

With that he stamped off. If he truly believed the globe was magic, how would I get him to leave it when the time came to escape from the Samoyeds? It was true the shaman allowed Georgi to hold it, but the shaman never let Georgi out of his sight unless the shaman had possession of the globe.

There was no time to think of what I might do, for we heard men shouting in the distance. Edeiko and the shaman appeared out of the forest, and behind them first one and then ten and then a hundred reindeer came straggling into camp, trailed by the herders urging them on. We all ran to meet them, the women calling out noisily, the children dancing about. In his hands the shaman held the globe.

Georgi gave me a triumphant look. "I told you it was magic," he said. "I told you so."

My heart sank. I did not see how I would ever

separate either the shaman or Georgi from the globe.

Still, I rejoiced at the herd's return, not only because it meant we could resume our march northward to Mama, but also because by now I had made many friends, and the troubles of the Samoyeds had become my troubles. I felt a part of the tribe. I no longer stood about but gathered firewood, knowing which branches burned well and which ones smoldered and smoked. While I still could not bring myself to eat the mess, I could mix a pudding of half-digested grass with just the right amount of blood and fat. I knew how to lay the reindeer hides across the tent poles and make neat rolls of the hides when we packed the carts to move on.

I was comfortable on the back of a reindeer and even had my favorite, which carried Tadibe and me. I was sure by her snuffling noise and the toss of her head that our reindeer recognized me when I strolled among the herd.

As Tadibe and I chattered, first in her language

and then in mine, I learned there was a young herder whom she hoped to marry. When she married, she would receive her own reindeer. Those reindeer would breed, and one day she would own a small herd. It was the first time I realized that some of the reindeer belonged to the women.

Together we picked wild cloudberries and blueberries and hunted for mushrooms. When their work was done, the women spent the summer evenings sewing, thankful for the white nights. When winter came, there would be no light for such work. Tadibe was clever with embroidery, and her boots and dresses were richly colored and thick with her handiwork. These skills, I learned, would get her a good husband. Tadibe taught me how to embroider. Though at first I was clumsy and my work crude, Tadibe never made fun of it but patiently showed me how to improve. After a bit I began to think it a lot like my painting. The needle was my brush and the colored threads my paint.

Georgi, too, found his place in the tribe. Language

made no difference in his friendship with the other boys his age. They played at lassoing one another, pretending they were reindeer, or if we were near the river, they would fish together. With his deeply tanned round face and black hair, you could hardly tell Georgi from the Samoyed children.

The old shaman loved to tell Georgi stories, which Edeiko translated. The shaman taught Georgi how to fish in the best spots and how to choose the best path for the reindeer. Each morning the shaman would take Georgi by the hand and, along with two or three of the herders, would walk a bit one way and then another. At last one path would be chosen over the other, and the shaman would explain the reason for the choice to Georgi. Georgi would nod his head wisely, as if he had known all along this was the path wide enough for the herd to pass through, with a patch of good grazing at its end.

The reindeer traveled along with us in a loose way, straggling here and there. When I questioned this,

Edeiko explained, "The reindeer like their freedom. If you pen them up or make them travel in a tight pack, they became unhappy and will not eat well." When I heard how much the reindeer valued their independence, I liked them even better. Still, the herders had to be watchful. If any of the herd came upon wild reindeer, they were likely to join them and wander away. In the winter months, when the Samoyeds began their travels to the south, the reindeer would be fat and clumsy from all the summer grazing. Then the tribe always traveled close to the river. If the reindeer were attacked by wolves, they could escape into the water.

The third week we reached the tundra. The land was like a drawing that had been erased. There was nothing but moss and lichen and tall grasses. What trees there were, dwarf willow and birch, were stunted, growing into twisted shapes. The reindeer gorged from morning to night on the mosses and lichens and grasses.

When Georgi asked Edeiko where all the trees had

gone, Edeiko drove a stick into the ground. He showed us that only a few inches down there was ice, ice like a cold hand that clutched at the roots of whatever dared stretch into its killing surface.

Because of the ice, the tent poles would not stick into the ground without much hammering, and you could feel the chill of the ice beneath your feet. Without trees the sun beat down upon us, and the mosquitoes were fierce, but the Samoyeds were happy. The lichens and mosses were what they had traveled for. This was where the herds of reindeer fattened, and that fat would help them survive the cruel Siberian winter.

I was happy too, for when I looked on the map, though I could not find exactly where we were, I saw that Dudinka was near the Arctic Circle, and I began to plan our escape.

It was the last day of July when the man with the little leather case visited the tribe. The day before, Edeiko had gone into a town to barter two reindeer for iron kettles and knives. He must have been seen by the authorities, for one of the Samoyeds ran up to the shaman to report that a government man and two soldiers could be seen in the distance approaching the tribe. Tadibe began to cry.

"Why are you crying?" I asked. "What will the man do?"

"Children away" was all I could understand through Tadibe's sobs. The other children were crying as well. Mothers clutched their young to them, wailing at the news of the man's coming. The shaman looked very angry.

I tried to find out from Edeiko what was happening.

"They have come to take the children. There is a law that all Samoyed children of school age must learn the Russian language. Our children will be sent far away to school. We will not see them for years. It has happened that way to other tribes."

"If they spoke Russian," I asked, "would they be taken?"

"No, no, but they speak no Russian, only the few words you have taught Tadibe."

"You must quickly hide the children," I said. "Send them out beyond the hills. Georgi and I will be your children." I arranged my scarf to cover my blond hair. From being outside all summer, my face was as brown as Tadibe's.

After a moment of thought Edeiko approached the shaman. There was a quick, loud discussion. Edeiko returned, looking worried.

"The shaman says you will tell your story to the men so that you can escape. Such a plan will only bring more trouble to us. We must hide you."

I dared to go to the shaman. "Tell him," I ordered Edeiko, "that he has my solemn promise that Georgi and I will not betray him. It's your only chance. Tell him I'm doing it for Tadibe."

The shaman frowned, but after a long moment he had all the school-aged children pulled from their mothers' arms and sent toward the hills. Only Tadibe remained. "I speak Russian now," she insisted.

I gave Edeiko a worried look. Before he could decide what to do, a man with a thin leather suitcase appeared, followed by two armed soldiers. They strode past the terrified men and women and approached the shaman. The man introduced himself as Comrade Boris. Edeiko translated the comrade's imperious demand to see the children.

Tadibe, Georgi, and I were pushed forward. I was sure Georgi and I, with our tanned faces and our boots and clothes of reindeer hide, would pass as children of the tribe.

The man looked about at the babies and toddlers and then at us. "Surely these are not all the school-aged children?" he asked.

Edeiko said, "There was an epidemic of fever, and we lost many of our children. Others were taken by the government in years past."

Comrade Boris looked uncertain. At last he said, "Then we must take these three. They will be taught

Russian. Stalin has ordered that everyone in this country must speak Russian so that our country can march forward."

"We do speak Russian," I said, coming up behind him.

Startled, the man spun around. "What! Where did you learn Russian?"

I pointed to Edeiko. "He taught us."

"You"—he pointed at Georgi—"what words do you know in Russian?"

"I know all the words," Georgi said. "I had them in spelling."

I stepped in front of Georgi to cut him off before he could mention his school. "Edeiko taught us spelling and writing as well, " I said.

"And you." He prodded Tadibe. "Let me hear you speak Russian."

I held my breath. "One, two, three, four, five, six, seven, eight, nine, ten," Tadibe recited. That morning I had taught her to count.

The comrade took three pieces of paper from his case and three pencils. "You will write what I tell you," he said.

Hastily Edeiko pointed to Tadibe. "This one has been blind from birth. She talks but she does not see to write."

The man gave Tadibe an uncertain look but only said to Georgi and me, "Write down, 'Stalin is our great father.'"

I saw that Georgi was about to say something. In a firm voice I ordered, "Write what the man says at once, Georgi."

"'Stalin is our great father who loves and protects his people.'"

Georgi glowered at me. Like Georgi, everything inside me wanted to shout that Stalin was a cruel and evil man who had taken away our parents and now wished to take away Tadibe and the other children.

"Write, Georgi," I ordered. I began to write as well. If I could save Tadibe and the other children, I didn't care that I was writing lies.

The man watched closely as we put the words down.

Georgi looked up. "We didn't have the word *protect*. It's not fair to give me that word."

"Hush, Georgi," I begged. "Sound it out." I pronounced the word carefully.

Georgi bit his pencil and frowned. At last he wrote *pratect*, using an *a* instead of an *o*, but the man did not seem to care. He only looked puzzled at how quickly we wrote.

At last he turned to Edeiko. "Very well—tell your shaman the children may stay. But next year the state will put your people and their herd of reindeer into one of the collective farms. There will be no more wandering about. All people must work together for the common good. Then all your children will be sent to a proper school."

Edeiko did not say a word.

"Tell him," the government man ordered.

Dragging his feet, Edeiko approached the shaman. He said some words to the shaman, who reacted by jumping to his feet and shouting at the government man.

"What does he say?" the comrade asked.

I could see that Edeiko was reluctant to repeat the shaman's angry words. At last he mumbled that the shaman had said reindeer must never be penned up for long periods, that they had to graze on the tundra, and that hay would never take the place of the lichen and moss they needed.

The comrade dismissed the words. "We have agricultural experts. They need no advice from you. Mark my words, by next year the reindeer and all your people will be behind a fence." With that he marched across the tundra toward the road, the soldiers trailing along behind him, rifles still drawn.

Tadibe rushed at me, throwing her arms around me and dancing about. "Marya!" she cried. "Good, good, good!" She added with a laugh, "Russian word."

When several hours passed and the men had not returned, the children were led back. The women were hugging their children. Most of them had not understood what had happened. They only knew that after talking with me, Comrade Boris and his soldiers had left and would not take away their children.

Edeiko led Georgi and me to the shaman. "He wishes to speak with you," Edeiko said. Edeiko's broad forehead was wrinkled. The corners of his mouth turned down. I wondered if something I had said had angered the shaman. Perhaps he was afraid we would escape after all and betray the children.

Instead, when we stood before him, the shaman solemnly handed Georgi his globe. "He says you are to keep it with you," Edeiko said. "Because you have saved our children from being sent away, you may have your freedom, and the boy may keep the little cottage with the falling snow."

Georgi looked from Edeiko to the shaman and back again. A wide smile crossed his face. Then, much to everyone's horror—for it was a great taboo to touch the shaman—Georgi threw his arms about the old man. Before he could catch himself, a smile opened like a flower across the shaman's face. I thought how sad it would be to be a shaman and never be touched in a friendly or loving way.

A moment later the smile disappeared and the shaman was his usual stern self, untangling himself from Georgi's crushing hug.

As we had traveled, we had kept away from the towns and villages, and I could no longer find our location on the map. Now that we were free to go, I asked Edeiko, "How much farther to Dudinka?" I thought it would be a week or more, and we would ask if we could stay with the tribe a little longer.

Edeiko smiled. "It is only two days' journey. The tribe will camp at a distance from the town."

I couldn't keep the excitement from my voice. "Will you go into the town, Edeiko?" I knew Edeiko was sent to do the bartering.

"Not this time. We have all we need, and the shaman is anxious to get to our summer camp."

"Will you take us close to the town?"

Edeiko sighed. "If you wish. The shaman has said you are to be free to go where you like."

"I think our mother is there, Edeiko." At last I was giving away our secret.

His eyes grew very wide. Hastily he turned to the shaman and the others. He must have told them what I had said, for they appeared excited for us.

The first day passed quickly, but that night neither Georgi nor I slept. Georgi wandered away from the shaman's tent and crawled into my tent, settling beside me.

"Will we really find Mama, Marya?" he whispered.

I could not honestly tell him we would. Months had passed since Mama's letter. She might have given up hope of hearing from us and gone away. All I could say was "I hope so, Georgi."

In the morning Edeiko came for us. Tadibe begged me not to leave. "Your people," she repeated over and over, pointing to herself and the other members of the tribe.

I could only shake my head and wipe away my tears.

There were many farewells, the men patting our heads, the women giving us food to take. When I offered to give back our boots, there were loud protests.

All this time the shaman said no word. He sat very still, his face composed into his usual stern expression, but to my amazement as he watched Georgi get ready to leave, I saw two tears roll down his cheeks. Georgi saw them too. He turned and ran toward the shaman, pressed the globe into his hands, and ran to catch up with us. When I looked back, I saw the shaman was holding the globe, but there was no pleased smile on his face. I did not think the tears had been for the loss of the globe.

CHAPTER ELEVEN

DUDINKA

As we grew close to Dudinka, we were amazed to see the houses were all suspended on concrete posts so that they looked like houses on stilts. "You cannot build on the permafrost," Edeiko explained. "The warmth from the house would melt the ice beneath it, and the house would sink."

Edeiko said that he must leave us there at the outskirts of the city and return to the tribe. We clung to him. He patted our heads and seemed as sorry to leave us as we were to have him go. We stood watching until he was no more than a small figure moving across the tundra.

Georgi, who was humming to himself, clung so tightly to my hand, I had to ask him to be a little more gentle. Dudinka appeared larger than I had imagined. We walked down what seemed to be the city's main street. People hurried by us, pausing only long enough to take in our Samoyed clothes and boots. Still, this was reindeer country, and it must not have been unusual to see Samoyeds in the city bartering their reindeer for goods. As for my blond hair, that was tucked under my scarf again.

I had Mama's address from the letter. Several times I stopped women with friendly faces to show them the address. After they got over their surprise at our Russian words, no one seemed to know where the address was located. At last a woman nodded.

"Yes, yes. It is two squares this way and ten squares that way. You can't miss it." The street was in a neighborhood of tiny shacks that tilted this way and that on their stilts. In the August heat the doors of the shacks were open.

There were no numbers on the huts, and I had to go from shack to shack, climbing ladders to get to the doors, where I would describe Mama. The people in the shacks looked at us suspiciously and shook their heads.

It was not until we came to the last shack that we found someone who recognized our description of Mama. A toothless man with a shiny bald head said, "This is the place, but the woman is long gone. I am cursed with the place now." When I asked if he knew where she had moved to, he shook his head. "No. I have no idea where she is." He stared at us. "What will you take for those boots?" He advanced toward us, a greedy look on his face. Pulling Georgi after me, I climbed down the ladder and ran away.

We had spent so long in coming to Dudinka, I did not see how Mama could not be there. Always in my mind she had been waiting for us, her arms out, a smile on her face, and now she had vanished. We were here and she was not. I hardly knew what to do next.

We had plenty of food from the tribe. When night came, we curled up near the river. The river in Dudinka was not the river we had followed—it was more a sea than a river. There were ships and barges everywhere, and overhead thousands of shrieking gulls.

We slept only a few hours. We had come more than a thousand miles, and it seemed we were as far from finding Mama as we had ever been. I had only the single ruble, and I knew the authorities would soon hear of two suspicious Samoyed children wandering about the city. They would surely arrest us. We could not even return to the tribe, for they were far away by now, in what direction I had no idea.

The next morning we waited what seemed to be forever for the stores to open. I took Georgi by the hand and, after once again getting up my courage, asked where the post office was. When we entered the post office, the postmistress stared at us, wondering no doubt why two Samoyed children not only spoke

Russian but were asking for a Russian woman as well.

Finally, after squinting for a long while at us through her small wire-framed glasses, she said, "A woman by that name comes here often asking for a letter. She was here only yesterday."

I could hardly breathe. "Where does she live?" I asked.

"I have no idea, but it must not be nearby, for she always looks tired and hot."

Mama was here after all! I wanted to throw my arms around the woman and dance her about the post office. Though I begged and begged, the woman could tell me nothing more.

I could hardly bear to think Mama might have been in the town with us only the day before. We might have passed close by her and never guessed. Waiting was impossible. We had to find her at once.

That night we looked for shelter. The ground by the river where we had slept the night before had been damp and cold from the icy layer that lay beneath it. At last we curled up in the entrance to the post office.

At least, I thought, we would be lying on ground over which Mama had walked.

In the morning I decided that each day we would walk in a different direction looking for Mama. West was the river, so we would explore the north, south, and east. We would begin with the east.

After a breakfast of dried cranberries and dried reindeer meat, we began to walk east toward the rising sun, following a narrow path that led through a scattering of wooden houses, some with chickens inside the house, and in one yard an unhappy reindeer. Georgi and I scraped up some moss and fed the poor beast until an angry man climbed down from his house, shouting at us.

The village huts became fewer until it seemed, with no trees and no houses, that Georgi and I were the only things sticking up on the earth.

Suddenly Georgi whispered, "Marya, Marya, look over there. The ground is moving." He caught at my skirt and held on.

It was true! Just beyond us the earth was moving.

It wriggled and surged, broke apart and came together. I heard myself shriek. For as far as I could see, a river of yellow-tannish animals, no larger than the palm of my hand, was running across our path, heading north. I knew what they were—lemmings. We had read in school how they traveled to the sea, where they drowned.

Overhead the sky was filled with eagles and vultures swooping down to clutch the animals in their talons. At the edges of the furry mass I saw a fox pluck one of the small animals. In the distance there was a gray shadow that might have been a wolf.

Georgi and I stood silent, hypnotized by the sight of so many thousands of animals. The first ones were nearing a shallow lake cut out of the tundra, but the animals weren't turning away. On they came, and with them the birds, swooping and diving. The first of the lemmings slipped into the water as if it were merely a continuation of the path. Some struggled and drowned. The rest hurried over the backs of the first wave. We stood by, not wanting to see but unable to look away.

When at last the lemmings had passed, there was nothing green to be seen anywhere. The animals had eaten every bit of moss and every blade of grass. We turned and made our way slowly back to Dudinka, so amazed by what we had seen, we could not find a word to say.

It was early afternoon. Georgi was looking hungrily into the window of a store. "Marya, you promised me cake." I fingered the ruble I still had in my pocket.

The shopkeeper was putting a tray of *piroshki* in the window. "Mama used to make some just like that," Georgi said. "Couldn't we have one?"

Recklessly I decided to spend a few kopecks to buy two. The *piroshki* would bring Mama closer. Cheese or bread would have lasted longer, but I could not help myself.

The shelves of the shop were nearly empty. There were a few jars of pickles, some hunks of hard cheese, a vinegar barrel, and a few fish whose pale, sunken eyes and bad smell told me they were yesterday's catch. With so much ice beneath us, I did not see why there should not be ice in the case.

The shopkeeper was handing back a basket to a woman. I could not see the woman's face, but her stooped shoulders and straggling hair, her shabby dress and slow movements, were that of an old woman.

The shopkeeper turned toward us. "What can I do for you?"

I pointed hungrily at the little meat pies in the window. "How much are the *piroshki*?" I asked.

"Five kopecks, and you'll never get fresher. Here is the woman who makes them. She has just brought a tray."

The woman turned to us for a moment, barely glancing at us. She gave us a sad smile, took up her basket, and was about to leave the store when the expression on our faces stopped her. She looked again.

Georgi and I could not move. We had come over a thousand miles but we could not take one step.

The woman who was Mama said in a cold voice, "I must be getting on." She turned and quickly left the shop.

I was sure she had recognized us. Even in our strange clothes, how could she not? Was it possible that she didn't want us there? I grabbed Georgi's hand and ran from the shop while the shopkeeper called after us, "What about the *piroshki*?"

Desperately we looked around. There was no sign of Mama.

"Here, Marya, Georgi, here."

Mama was motioning to us from the back of the store. We ran to her and were crushed in her arms. We could not hold her tightly enough or stop kissing her. Our faces were wet from her tears and ours. We would let one another go for a moment to get our breath, and then in seconds we were clinging to one another.

At last Mama released us, still holding tightly to

our hands as though we might disappear altogether if she let go.

"I dared not let the shopkeeper know about you. She is a suspicious woman, and I have seen her talking with the policemen in the town.

"Now, quickly, we'll go to Ludmilla's. Her little house is on the outskirts of the town. On the way you must tell me how it is that you are dressed like the Samoyeds and what miracle has brought you here."

"Who is Ludmilla?" I asked.

"She is an angel," Mama said. "When I first arrived in Dudinka, I had no place to live but a filthy hovel in the town, and even there I could not find enough money to put food in my mouth. One day I saw an elderly woman struggling with her baskets of groceries. I helped her carry them to her home. I have been with her ever since. I keep her house and I have made a vegetable garden for her. Baking and selling the *piroshki* gives me a little money to help with the expenses."

"But will she let us stay there too?" I asked.

"Yes, yes, she knows all about the two of you. She will think you have dropped from heaven, as indeed you have. What miracle brought you to Dudinka?"

"We followed the river and then we rode a reindeer," Georgi said. And so we began our story. But there was more to tell than even the long walk allowed for: By the time we reached Ludmilla's house, we had come only to the shaman and the globe.

"And can you find me another, Mama?" Georgi asked. "I gave mine to the shaman so he wouldn't be sad."

"Yes, Georgi, if I have to travel all over Siberia."

I saw that the small cottage stood, like all the houses in Dudinka, on stilts. At the door of the cottage was the figure of Ludmilla, her hand shading her eyes, watching us. As we drew closer, I could see she was very old, stooped and wrinkled, with long white hair that hung in wisps to her shoulders. She held a rabbit in each arm.

Mama said, "Ludmilla's husband died two years ago. He worked on the barges that go up and down the river. You will see, she is kindness itself."

Ludmilla hobbled down the ladder. "What is this? What have you found? Katya, can it be? Have our prayers been answered? Why are they dressed like that? Quickly, come into the house and let me give you some cool water. We have our own spring. You have never tasted such water, so cold it's like swallowing an icicle. And bread. I have just baked bread. And there is jam." She turned to Georgi. "Your mama says you like jam."

The little cottage was no more than two small rooms, but it was spotlessly clean, with flowered curtains at the windows and crocheted rugs on the wood floor. In one corner a candle burned in front of an icon of St. Vladimir. A basket of knitting lay next to a chair. There was a large stove for cooking and for heating the little cottage. Shelves ran along the stove. "Those shelves will be our beds in the winter," Mama said. Beside the stove was a neat pile of kindling and a barrel of flour. Delicious smells came from the oven.

Even in my imagination I could not have invented so perfect a place.

Georgi said, "If there were only snow falling, Mama, this would be the cottage in my little globe."

Mama laughed. "There will be snow soon enough, Georgi."

Ludmilla put down the rabbits and opened the oven door. Using her apron as a potholder, she snatched out a loaf of bread, sliced it, and spread it thickly with jam. Mama poured water for us that was so cold that, hot as we were, we could hardly swallow it. All the while four rabbits ran about the house, crawling under beds and hopping from one room to the other.

"Now, now," Ludmilla scolded them. "Settle down or we'll have one of you for dinner."

We were not long with Ludmilla before I realized there was no one more tenderhearted. Though she raised the rabbits for food and threatened the rabbits daily to turn them into a stew, the rabbits were never eaten, at least by her, for she made extra money by selling them in the town.

As soon as we had settled down at the table, we had to begin our story from the beginning and tell it all again. She listened with tears rolling down her cheeks, murmuring over and over, "A miracle, a miracle from St. Vladimir."

"Never a day passed," she said, "without your mother and me praying to him."

"And we must pray to him still," Mama said, "until Papa is with us."

It was the first time she had spoken about Papa. I hurried to tell her, "We met a doctor who was going to the coal-mining camps in Vorkuta. He was a good man and he promised to look for Papa, but I couldn't tell him what camp Papa was in." It was our only sad time that day, for the miracle of our finding one another made us believe that someday we would see Papa.

THE STRANGER

That evening we slept in beds for the first time in two months—and not only in beds, but on soft feather beds, for Ludmilla kept chickens. Nothing could have been better than the softness of the bed and Mama right there in the same room with us.

We awoke to hear Mama and Ludmilla whispering to each other. When they saw we were awake, Mama said, "We have been talking, and we have decided that we must tell anyone who asks that you are Ludmilla's grandchildren come to stay with her because her daughter is not well.

"I must report regularly to the town's Communist

Party chairman," she went on. "He is a hard man, and if he discovered you had run away from Leningrad, he might arrest you."

Though Mama's words frightened me, I soon put them aside, for Ludmilla had prepared an enormous breakfast for us. There were fresh eggs. I had two, and Georgi three. After breakfast Mama showed us about. I would feed the hens, she said, and since Georgi, like Ludmilla, was never without a rabbit in his arms, he was to feed the rabbits and clean their cages.

"I have never trusted anyone with my rabbits," Ludmilla told Georgi, "even your mother. But I can see the little pets have taken to you."

At the foot of the ladder there was a garden growing in tubs of precious earth, with potatoes, onions, carrots, and the largest cabbages I had ever seen. "The season is short," Mama said, "but there is no night, so the cabbages never stop fattening."

The little house with Mama was a paradise. We were like so many peas in a pod. The smallness of the house made everything cozy. Ludmilla had her own tiny room. Mama, Georgi, and I all slept in the other room, so we were always together. Mama taught me how to make *piroshki*, and each day we walked into town with our fresh batch for the bakery. After Mama collected her money, we strolled along the river watching the barges and fishing boats, thinking of the walks we had taken along the Neva in Leningrad. Georgi brought his fishing line and sat on the wharves next to tanned and wrinkled fishermen who delighted in the fierce way he fished. Sometimes they let him pull in a big fish on their own, stronger lines.

While Georgi fished and I drew pencil sketches of the fishing boats, Mama sat looking out at the harbor. I knew she was hoping against hope that Papa would step off of one of the incoming boats.

After Mama bought whatever supplies we needed with the few kopecks the *piroshki* earned, we started for Ludmilla's, where we were welcomed home and urged to tell of all we had seen in the town.

The days were much the same, with only small surprises: new rabbits, a yellow-and-black butterfly, excitement in Dudinka because the salmon were coming up the river to spawn and there were as many as you wished to eat. The greatest surprise of all came on the first day of September. We stopped, as we always did, at the post office. Our visits had always been useless, but this day Mama was handed a letter. She said nothing, but her hand was trembling. Georgi and I followed her outside. We hurried to a spot along the river where we would not be noticed. Mama carefully opened the letter. She read it once and, wiping away tears, gave it to us with a trembling hand.

Dear Ekaterina Ivanovna,

It was my great pleasure to become acquainted with your daughter and son. I left them in the best of health and pray that they are now with you. I have never known two

*children with a better idea of where they
were going.*

*I am writing to tell you that another
member of your family is on his way.*

*My wife joins me in wishing your family
well. Please tell your son that my boys send
him their greetings.*

A friend

We knew at once that the letter was from Dr.
Glebov. It was a short letter, for Dr. Glebov was careful to say as little as he could. We hurried to the cottage and, scrambling up the ladder, we held the letter
out to Ludmilla.

"It is your papa. He is coming." Ludmilla threw
her arms around us. "Another miracle from St.
Vladimir."

Each day we instructed the postmistress as to
where we lived. "If anyone asks for Ekaterina Ivanovna, she is at old Ludmilla's cottage."

"Yes, yes." The postmistress looked at us suspiciously, but we didn't care. All we cared about was finding Papa. We met all the steamboats, but Papa was not on them.

In late September we awakened more than once to find the windows of the cottage iced over. The tender beans had long since been picked and put up, and the cabbages were in a barrel of brine, but the turnips and carrots were left in the dirt to sweeten. The rabbits had been brought inside. Since there were no trees on the tundra, Mama, Georgi, and I had met the barges carrying firewood up the river. We took the firewood home in a wagon, and now the ground beneath the stilts was nearly covered by the heaps of firewood Mama's *piroshki* had paid for.

October came, and now there was always a fire in the woodstove. A crust of ice crept over the river. There were fewer barges. The long white nights were over.

One morning I opened the door of the cottage to

see fresh footprints in the snow. My heart began to race. I knew that Mama and Ludmilla had not been outside. I was afraid someone might be spying on us. I knew that I must call Mama. I started to close the door when a bearded man, dirty and dressed in rags, climbed up the ladder. I cried out and tried to slam the door on him.

"Maryushka."

It was Papa's pet name for me.

Georgi and Mama and Ludmilla hurried to the door. We crowded around Papa until he begged us to let him breathe. At last he was settled on a chair placed next to the stove, a glass of hot tea in his hand. Mama, Georgi, and I were at his feet. Ludmilla stood close beside us, crying, a rabbit under each arm. We could not look at or touch Papa enough.

As happy as we were to have Papa with us, our hearts were broken when we saw how thin he was. His cheeks were sunken, his fingers twisted. There were bruises on his face, and he coughed until we thought he would choke. Most frightening of all was the expression in his eyes. All the laughter was gone. He was looking beyond us to something frightening and terrible.

We all took turns telling our stories. Georgi and I told Papa of our trip. We told him of Old Savoff and of the bear and the Samoyeds. Papa told his own story.

"I was no more sick than the other prisoners, but Dr. Glebov watched over me, reporting me too ill to work and ordering that I be put in the hospital. Through some miracle he found a passport for me, and though he had hardly enough for his family, he gave me money for passage on a freighter.

"After coming to me in the night to alert me, he summoned the guard at the prison hospital to help him with a sick patient. While the guard was busy, I escaped and made my way to the sea. The next morning I was on a freighter that sailed to Dudinka."

Over and over I blessed the doctor for what he had done for Papa, and was ashamed that I had ever suspected him.

As Papa told his story, the coughing grew worse. Mama and Ludmilla made up a bed for Papa on the stove shelf, where it was warm. He managed a little broth and then fell into a deep sleep. Mama never left his side, and many times during that night Georgi and I awoke and tiptoed to the stove to be sure Papa was still there.

All Papa's strength had been used up in finding us. He lay in bed or propped up by pillows in a chair, coughing and coughing. He hated to let Mama or Georgi or me out of his sight. When Mama took the *piroshki* into town, one of us would stay with Papa. All the time Mama was gone, Papa watched the path looking for her return.

He was fond of the rabbits. It pleased Ludmilla to see how he would take one on his lap and pet its long silky ears. "So soft, so gentle. I had never thought to hold something so soft again, or to see something so gentle." He would sigh, and his eyes would get a haunted look. We all knew he was thinking of the camp, but he would not speak of it.

It was in late October, when we were in town buying enough flour to last the winter, that we saw a cart drawn by four reindeer and piled high with bear and seal skins. There were Edeiko and two of the other Samoyeds. They had already sold some of their reindeer to the butcher and were now busy trading furs for supplies.

There was a rush of words as we told Edeiko that our papa was back, but very sick, and how he was coughing and coughing. Edeiko listened carefully, asking where our cottage was. He said the tribe was readying for their return trip south. I sent my love to Tadibe and made sure the reindeer that had carried me was not at the butcher shop. At last we said good-bye.

The next morning there was a knock on the door. Edeiko and the sleigh were outside. The sleigh was piled high.

"From the shaman," Edeiko said, "and from Tadibe and the women." There were winter boots and gloves, and for Papa a parka ingeniously made with a hood and a flap that you could pull up to cover part of your face. There was half a reindeer to feed us, cut into haunches and chops. "Not your reindeer," Edeiko assured me. "The summer feeding has been very good. The reindeer are fat." Edeiko smiled. "The shaman says the little globe with the snow has brought the tribe good luck."

Ludmilla stood by, her hands raised, her mouth open in astonishment at the gifts, while a half dozen rabbits got under everyone's feet.

When the Samoyeds left, we were so overcome with wonder at our treasures, we could hardly talk. Finally Mama and Ludmilla prepared the reindeer, cutting it into manageable pieces and hanging it outside, where it would remain frozen until it was needed.

As Georgi and I tried on our new caps and boots, Papa exclaimed over and over, "What good people, what kind people." Tears came into his eyes. "First the doctor and now these people. I never thought to believe in human kindness again."

I think it was the kindness that gave him the courage at last to tell us of the camp, for it was the evening of the Samoyeds that he gathered us around him.

"I didn't want you to know such cruelty, such inhumanity existed," he said to Georgi and me. "But I know now how much goodness you have seen. If I tell you of evil, you will have experienced good, and it will protect you from believing too badly of your fellow man."

I knew what Papa meant, for I thought every day of those who had helped Georgi and me on our journey—the Glebovs, Old Savoff's wife, and the Samoyeds. With all the evil around us, we had found people to trust. They had been like the shelter of pine boughs Georgi and I had built to keep us safe from the dangerous storm that raged all around us.

Mama begged. "Misha, say no more. Such memories will only trouble you."

"No, Katya," Papa said. "The day may come when our beloved Russia comes to her senses. When that happens, people will forget. They will want to put these terrible times behind them, but what of the families torn apart and the lives lost? If our stories are not passed on, who will remember us? How will we guard against such things happening again? No, hard as it will be to listen to, Marya and Georgi must hear the truth.

"We were taken from the Kresti Prison to the train station and thrown into boxcars," Papa said.

I thought of the boxcars Georgi and I had seen in the station and shuddered. Papa might have been in one of them.

"After a day's journey we felt the cars being shunted from one engine to another, and we guessed we had arrived in Moscow and were headed for Siberia. We had no food or water. When the train paused at a station, we pounded on the doors but no one came. At last, after two days, the doors were opened and we were given pails of water and loaves of stale bread. We were like animals fighting over the water. That was the worst part—how inhuman they had made us. After the trains, we were put into barges and taken on the river, which was close to the camps. We were lucky we didn't freeze to death before we reached the camps.

"We were sent to work in a coal mine," Papa said. "They put us in cages and sent us a mile under the ground. We worked in the dark. It was as if someone had stolen the very sun from the sky. We were covered with coal dust. It got under our nails and into our skin. We breathed it and ate it. They took away our names and gave us numbers, so there were times when we could not recall our own names. In the barracks we were packed so tightly together, you soon forgot where the other person left off and you began. Everyone was sick: typhus, pneumonia, tuberculosis. Every night was a terrible symphony of coughs. Every day someone was carried out, and every day a new prisoner arrived to take his place.

"When all the coal was taken from the large tunnels, they sent us into the small channels, only large enough for one man. You could not stand up but stayed all day crouching on your knees trying to find enough room to swing your pick. When you did manage to chip out a bit of coal, you had to dodge the sharp pieces that flew out at you. We all had cuts, and some of the men were blinded in one eye."

Papa's voice grew even weaker. We could hardly make out his words. Mama begged him to stop, but he would not.

"There is only one thing more to tell. It is what convinced me to leave." He waited a moment to gather his strength. "On a day I will never forget, there was a noise, a muffled shrieking noise, like a hand placed over a screaming man's mouth. Suddenly everything began to shake. Rocks fell on us. The world was coming apart. A section of the mine collapsed. We escaped, but there were a dozen men working in the part of the mine that was sealed off by the collapse. Some of us volunteered to go down and dig them out. It didn't matter to us that we were risking our lives—what were our lives in that place, that we would not willingly have risked them? It was not allowed. They had set a goal—so many cars of coal were needed. The rescue would have meant taking a day or two away from our work. Instead of saving the men, they walled up the seam where the men had been working so no one could hear their cries.

"When that happened, I went to Dr. Glebov. 'Help me escape,' I begged. He told me I was not well enough, that I would never survive such a journey. 'Then I will escape without your help,' I said. He knew that would be certain death, but he saw how desperate I was. Finally he agreed to help me."

We could hardly bear to hear Papa's terrible story, but we suffered it, for the telling made Papa better, as if some poisonous snake that had been coiled inside him had crawled off forever. He didn't get stronger, but he took a greater interest in things, chatting with Ludmilla about her rabbits and making plans with Mama for Christmas.

We were all shut into the cottage together against the Siberian winter. The windows were coated with frost, and a seal of ice had to be broken to open the door. On some days it was so cold that when we went out of doors, our eyelids froze together.

With no trees for shelter, the Siberian winds were like a great beast shaking and rattling our cottage. We huddled around the stove, where a pan of snow was always melting. The sun rose late and set in the afternoon, so our lives were lived by the light of candles and lanterns and by the stove's firelight.

Still, I was happy, for everywhere I looked, Papa and Mama were there. The Siberian winter was terrible to us but nothing to Ludmilla, who always had some tale of colder winters and stronger winds. "This is nothing," she would say when the snows came and the winds howled. And then would come the story of a stronger storm or a colder night.

Christmas arrived in a fall of snow. When I peeked outside, the world was a white blur. Mama told us of her Christmas in the tsar's palace, of the huge tree in the palace hall decorated with candies and gilded nuts and lit with hundreds of small candles. "On Christmas Eve sleighs carried us across the snow to church. I can still hear the sleigh bells. The tsar and the empress stood at the entrance of the church while the people came to bow to the tsar and kiss the empress's hand. And afterward, what a feast we had!"

On Christmas morning we all knelt before the icon of St. Vladimir and said our prayers. Mama had bought me a paint set and paper. For Georgi there was a package wrapped in store paper. It was a glass globe. Inside the globe was a small cottage on which the snow fell gently.

Georgi had written the story of the bear that the shaman had told and made it into a book for Papa, who had said how much he missed his books. I had embroidered a scarf for Mama in the pattern Tadibe had taught me. For Ludmilla Mama had knitted a warm shawl, and I had made the fringes. We all said it was a perfect Christmas.

At noon we had our own feast of borscht made with cabbage, carrots, and onions; a fine roast of reindeer; and *kutya*, made with poppy seeds and honey. For dessert there were *blini*, thin pancakes spread with jam made from wild berries. Ludmilla placed a bit of straw on the table to remind us of the manger in which the Christ child was born. In the evening we all sang carols by the light of the stove.

As the winter went on, Georgi and I grew less afraid of the ice and snow. We put on the Samoyeds' gifts and wandered out into the half-light of the day. How strange it was to discover in the snow the tracks of small creatures running about. Sometimes we saw a hawk or an owl and we felt less alone, less as though we were marooned on an ice floe. Once we saw an arctic fox, his white coat no more than a movement of white against the white snow.

March came, and then April. The days grew longer; the icicles that decorated the cottage dripped to nothing. The frost on the windows was no longer thick enough to draw pictures in. At any moment you could look up and see returning birds—hawks and gulls, lapwings and falcons and, once, perched on the roof of the cottage like a feathered ghost, a snowy owl. As it grew warmer, mysterious little pools and ponds seeped onto the surface of the tundra. Georgi tried fishing in them, but there were no fish, and in a day or two they would disappear. Papa said it was the ice melting beneath the land.

The kitchen was filled with the fragrance of *piroshki*. We began making regular visits again to the town with our baskets. Ludmilla started radish and lettuce seeds and planted them in pots on a sunny windowsill. One morning a seedling appeared, the first green thing we had seen in months. Georgi ran to show it to Papa, who held the pot with its green seedling in his hands for a long time.

There was a pocket-sized porch, and when it was warm enough, Papa, wrapped in a blanket, loved to sit outside in the sun. But as the days grew warmer and lighter, Papa grew weaker. Mama seldom left his side. Each morning as soon as my eyes opened, I looked to see if Papa was all right. Often I would wake in the middle of the night to find Mama and Papa deep in conversation. Almost always they were whispering about long-ago times and memories of Leningrad, which they always thought of as St. Petersburg.

"What wouldn't I give to see our beloved city once more, Katya," Papa said. That gave me the idea. I whispered to Georgi and Ludmilla. That evening after dinner I hurried into Ludmilla's tiny room and closed the door. All evening I painted, and the next evening as well.

On the afternoon of the third day, when Mama and Papa went to sit outside, Georgi, Ludmilla, and I got busy. We pushed and pulled the tables and chairs until we had a clear path through the room. Up went the sign I had painted that said NEVSKY PROSPEKT. Two chairs were placed on a table, and Ludmilla draped them with a blue cloth while I pinned on paper squares for windows and Georgi rolled paper into white pillars to decorate our Winter Palace. Farther along the path a blue rug became a canal. Beside the canal we fashioned a cathedral from the firebox. The bread bowl was painted in bright colors and turned upside down to make the dome. Off to one side I pinned all the drawings I had made of the Summer Garden, with its flowers and fountains and wide green lawns. By the stove Ludmilla set up a little table and two chairs. A white cloth was on the table, and a sign overhead read TEAROOM.

Georgi opened the door and called, "Welcome to St. Petersburg."

I led Mama and Papa inside while Ludmilla brushed one of the rabbits off the tearoom table. At first, when I saw them break into tears, I thought we had done something to make them sad, but I was wrong, for they were laughing as well as crying. They walked down the Nevsky Prospekt admiring the palace and the cathedral. With a sweep of his arm, Papa seated Mama in the tearoom and settled down next to her. Georgi, with an apron around his waist, brought glasses of tea, and Ludmilla proudly produced a plate of fancy cookies she had baked while Mama was taking her *piroshki* into the village. When they had finished their tea, Papa said, "And now for a stroll in the garden." Arm in arm they walked by my paintings, Mama commenting, "My, the geraniums are superb this year," while Papa agreed, "They have never looked so lovely."

After that afternoon Papa seemed better for a few days, but soon the coughing grew worse and Papa could not eat. It was a soft night in May when I heard him whisper to Mama, "I could not leave you alone in the cold and darkness of winter." When the first wildflowers were blooming on the tundra, Papa died.

Mama gathered Georgi and me in her arms. We cried for a very long time while Ludmilla patted us gently to console us. At last Ludmilla went into town to find a priest she knew, who was in hiding from the Communists and working as a shoemaker.

"He does not dare give us a real funeral," Ludmilla said, "but he will surely say some prayers." That night we followed the custom and stayed up all night to pray. The next morning I went out on the tundra to gather wildflowers—buttercups, primroses, and cowslips for Papa. Beneath the thin soles of my boots I felt the coldness of the ice under the tundra's surface. I knew that was how it would always be for me. Beneath whatever happiness came to me would be this icy coldness of Papa's death.

That day the shoemaker came, and there were more prayers. Then Papa was taken away.

After Papa died, we hardly left one another's sight. Georgi and I walked into town with Mama on her way to the bakery. She would go with us to the river.

We would meet the fishing boats and barter for salmon or cod. When the whaling ships arrived, everyone rushed down to the pier to see the bits and pieces of the great beasts that were left on the boats. The harbor was crowded now with barges and freighters. Steamboats came and went. There were rumors of a prison camp near Dudinka, and one day we saw prisoners in chains being led off a steamboat. Mama sank down on a bench. Her hands were trembling, and tears streamed from her eyes. "Poor Russia," she said over and over. "Russia is devouring her children."

There were happier days. Squirrels chased one another over the tundra. The new rabbits frisked about in their pens, giddy with being in the open air. New heads of cabbage like green roses thrived in the long days of sunlight. The birds returned one by one, and then one hundred by one hundred.

In the long, light evenings we would take the chairs onto the tiny porch and Mama would tell stories of her days in the palace.

"Can such things be?" Ludmilla would exclaim.

Sometimes Mama would look off into the distance. We knew then that she was thinking of Papa.

We were all changed by Papa's death. Ludmilla spent more time fussing over her rabbits. She would take them in her arms and croon, "Poor things, poor things." Mama was quieter. When she spoke, it was often about the old days, when she and Papa were young. Georgi had decided he was the man of the family and was bossy around the house, but all I thought about was how we might escape Siberia.

At night I would retrace the long trip we had made. One day Mama's exile would be over. Then Mama and Georgi and I would travel along the river, over the tundra and then into the forest, and finally back to the city of Krasnoyarsk and onto the train that would take us to St. Petersburg. All the Comrade Tikonovs and all the Comrade Stalins would not keep us out of our city. Night after night I made the trip, until each mile was familiar and a thousand miles were no more than a step.

GLOSSARY

babushka: grandma, old woman

blini: little pancakes

borscht: beet soup

isbas: the small wooden homes of Siberia

kopeck: a small coin; one hundred kopecks to a ruble

kutya: a porridge made of barley, honey, and nuts

makivnek: a raisin cake

malshyka: a brat

molodyets: well done!

NKVD: People's Commissariat of Internal Affairs; the Soviet secret police.

piroshki: small pies filled with cheese or meat

ruble: monetary sum

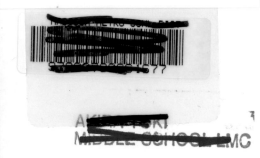